## AN AVALON HISTORICAL ROMANCE

## THE BETTIN' KIND
### *A Morgan Family Romance*

Nancy J. Parra

Amelia Morgan dreams of a handsome prince who would take one look at her and fall in love. Together they would breed a dynasty of magnificent horses and live happily ever after. What she never counted on was her baby brother losing her beloved stallion to a slick card shark. Desperate not to lose her dream, she gambles that the threat of marriage would cause the card shark to cut and run rather than go through with a hasty marriage to a total stranger.

Alex Laird is no dummy. He calls Amelia's bluff, fully expecting her to jilt him at the altar. Then the question of the horse's ownership would be indisputably his.

These two stubborn foes go through with a hasty marriage, neither willing to let go of their claim to the horse. Stuck with each other for the time being, each comes up with a plan to secure their future. Unfortunately, their goals are once again at odds. For a while, Alex decides an annulment is the answer to their predicament. Amelia takes a different tact. She believes the only way to see her dream come true is to make Alex fall in love with her. The struggles that ensue becomes more than a battle of wills. It becomes a battle of the heart where dreams are won and lost at the turn of a card.

# THE
# BETTIN' KIND

•

# Nancy J. Parra

*AVALON BOOKS*
NEW YORK

PRINTED IN THE UNITED STATES OF AMERICA
ON ACID-FREE PAPER
BY HADDON CRAFTSMEN, BLOOMSBURG, PENNSYLVANIA

For Phyllis Travers, Debbie Zellner, and everyone at Guest Communications. Thank you for your friendship, love, and support without which I wouldn't be the person I am today.

## Chapter One

"**I**'m in big trouble."

Amelia Morgan shook her head in disbelief and planted her gloved hands on her hips. "What did you do now?"

"I lost Applegate in a card game."

"You can't lose Applegate," she said firmly. "He doesn't belong to you." Henry sat on a tack bench next to Applegate's stall and he banged his dark handsome head against the wall.

"I know." Henry buried his head in his hands. "Papa's going to kill me."

Resigned, Amelia sat down next to her brother and took off her leather riding gloves. "Start at the beginning and tell me everything."

"I was suckered in," Henry said. "I sat down to play with the usual fellows except there was this new guy. He seemed to know what he was doing. Nice guy actually."

"Henry."

"He suckered me, Amelia, I swear. I was on a winning streak, a big winning streak. The guy was a good player but I was better."

1

"He wanted you to think you were better," Amelia said. She knew the type. Gambling was a family affair and every Morgan had learned how to play card games at an early age. They also knew every sucker trick there was. Papa was sure that if they were informed they couldn't be swindled. "You started to lose."

"I lost a little, but didn't suspect anything because I was right back on my streak."

"What did he wager?"

"Oh, Amelia, you should have seen it. The most beautiful two-man racer. I swear it had gold and mahogany trim. The leather seats were cushioned with gold buttons."

"Papa has a carriage."

"Not like this one. I've never seen anything like it. Even better it had never been raced."

"Why does he have it, if he doesn't race it?"

"He said he won it."

Amelia smacked her brother upside his head. "That right there was a big red flag."

"I know, I know," Henry said and rubbed his head. He banged the back of his head against the stable wall again in a poor attempt to knock some sense into it. "I was winning."

"*Was* being the key word."

"He wiped me out. I've got nothing left to buy Applegate back. Papa won't be home for at least a month and I don't know what to do."

Amelia took a deep breath and stood up. Problem-solving was what she did best. She just wished she didn't have to do it so often. "We'll have to go down there and talk to this fellow. He'll have to understand that you don't own Applegate."

"He won't understand," Henry said, his tone more certain than she liked. "There are rules to card games, Sis. A man's word is a man's word and I gave him my word on Applegate."

"You are not a *man*," she said and shot him a sidelong look. "You're seventeen."

"I'll be eighteen next month."

"A man would not gamble away something that isn't his," she said firmly and pulled her gloves back on. "Come on, take me to this fellow and we'll see what we can do."

"I'm supposed to meet him down by the stables at four."

She checked the dainty watch pinned to her riding jacket. It was 3:45. "We'll come up with something on the way there," she said and strode toward the street. "There has to be something you own that is worth as much to this man as my prize stallion."

"I do have a new pair of six-shooters," he said. "Maybe he'll take them."

"I have a feeling he's going to want more than that. Applegate is worth a lot in breeding stock alone."

"Maybe he'll take them as collateral," Henry said hopefully. He put his hands in his pockets. "I can take a couple of jobs down at the mill to earn the rest."

"That might work," she said. "Let's hope your swindler is a considerate man. Did he seem like the considerate type to you?"

"He seemed the swindling type to me."

"No, he didn't or you wouldn't have gotten caught!" It made Amelia angry that someone had taken advantage of her brother. He was just a boy, a rather big boy to be sure, but there were times when his head didn't keep up with his body. She prayed silently that this would change in the next few years.

She glanced at him. He ran his big hand through his hair and looked sheepish. It would change, she knew. Henry was the best and the brightest of the Morgan bunch. All he needed was time to mature. Right now they didn't have that time.

She thought about her possessions. She had a string of

pearls her mother had left her. They were South Pacific
pearls and worth enough to help certainly, but not enough to
pay the man off.

Maybe he would negotiate a trade. She doubted it. True
card sharks were rarely up for negotiation. She took a deep
breath of the sweet fall air and sighed. If it came down to it,
she'd simply have to engage the fellow in a game of cards
and win back the horse.

It was well known around town that Henry was a gifted
card player. What wasn't as well known was Amelia was better. She had the knack, her father said. She had never been
tested outside her home because men didn't gamble with
women, but Amelia didn't lose hope at that thought. Any
man who would swindle a young boy out of a horse that
clearly did not belong to him, just might play a game of
cards with a woman.

If that was the case, their problems were solved. She simply had to beat him.


Alex Laird was a cynic and he knew it. He'd been around
the town too many times not to believe the worst in people.
He leaned against the shingled stable and watched for the
boy, his hat drawn low over his face. He rested his left foot
against the back of the barn and crossed his arms.

He glanced at his pocket watch. 4:00 P.M. The boy was not
going to show. Anger and bitterness filled him and he spit to
express it but he kept his face expressionless. He had learned
long ago that it was best to appear calm. Then no one knew
for sure what you were thinking. It kept people from making
assumptions.

The funny thing was, most people weren't hard to figure
out. They wore their thoughts on their faces. They gave away
their feelings with a tilt of the head, or a flick of the wrist.
That was why Alex had become so good at cards. He'd

learned to read people and he'd learned what not to give away.

He shook his head and pushed away from the building. What he needed now was a good kick in the pants. He had known better than to draw the boy into the game, but heck, the kid was cocky, way too cocky for his own good. He was bound to learn his lesson sooner or later. Alex figured he might as well be the one to teach the kid. No one else in this small town was going to. The kid had skill and luck. All he had to do was learn to curb his attitude.

But the lesson was turning on Alex. He should have known that horse didn't belong to the kid. He should have demanded the animal the moment he laid down his winning hand. But the kid had looked so shocked that when he stammered about needing a little time, Alex had taken pity and given it to him.

It never paid to take pity. It always got Alex in trouble. Now he was going to have to go look for the kid. He hated this part, when he'd have to draw his gun and make it clear that payment was due.

He heaved a sigh, adjusted his gun belt and stepped out into the street where he was nearly run over by a little bit of a thing who was too busy scolding someone to watch where she was going.

She bounced right off of him and Alex put out his hands to catch her.

"Oh, my. I beg your pardon," she said.

Alex found himself looking into the bluest eyes he'd ever seen in his life. They were rimmed by thick black lashes and were as deeply mysterious as the ocean. Horn-rimmed glasses served only to magnify their beauty. They drew him in like the tide, but he let her go as if she had stung him. "Ma'am."

"I'm so sorry, I didn't see you," she said and then had the audacity to brush off his jacket as if she had left a mark.

Alex watched her small gloved hands run down his chest and felt a strange prickling on the back of his neck. "Enough." He caught her hands and gently pushed them off him.

"I'm sorry. I usually don't leave a dusty mark," she said. "But I had just come back from riding when Henry needed my immediate attention."

"Henry?"

"My brother," she said and waved her hand in his general direction.

Only then did Alex notice the boy. He stood beside her with his hands in his pockets and a sheepish look on his face.

"You involved your sister?" Alex asked the boy. He could not believe the cocky card player would hide behind a woman's skirts. This one took the cake.

"I had to involve her," Henry said. "Applegate is Amelia's dowry."

Alex turned his attention back on the girl. She was older than the boy, but not too far out of school herself. "You came for the horse?"

"Yes," she said calmly.

"You can't have him."

"Applegate is my dowry. Therefore I need him."

"I don't care about your needs," Alex said and crossed his arms. "The animal is mine. I won him fair and square."

"My father gave Applegate to me."

He looked from the gal to her brother. "Where's your father? I want to speak to him."

"You can't. He's in Tennessee," she said. From her tone of voice it was clear her frustration had deepened. "When it comes to that horse, you have to speak to me."

Alex was in no mood to mess around with a determined little gal. The horse was his. "Let's take this to the sheriff."

"Wait," the boy said. "I don't think the sheriff needs to be involved."

"I do," Alex said at the same time Amelia did. It seemed that, at least in this one instance, they were of like minds. "Fine, let's go."

The sheriff's office was at the end of the block. Alex waved toward it. He figured it didn't hurt to be a gentleman for the moment. It would be a different story once the sheriff got involved.

That little gal raised her nose in the air and brushed passed him. She was small and came up to his shoulder, but there was something about her that held his attention.

Maybe it was the auburn hair that peeked out from under her bonnet. Or maybe the sweet smell of peppermint that followed in her wake. It was clear the family had money. Her riding outfit was finely tailored to show off her youthful curves. The deep blue of her jacket matched the ridiculous hat she wore. Was that an ostrich feather sticking out the top?

Alex shrugged and followed her. It didn't matter. She was a woman and he knew better than to do business with a woman, lady or not.

He eyed the boy. Henry slunk along beside her. It was clear all his cockiness had left him. Good. By the time this business was settled the boy would see you don't bet things that aren't yours.

Alex held the door open and Amelia eyed him for a moment before she stepped inside. Her look said, "Now you'll see." Alex shook his head. He hated to ruin her day, but it was time she learned that the law was on his side in this matter.

They stepped into the center of the log cabin that served as the jail and Alex had a moment of regret. It smelled of old coffee and a good cigar, far better than the saloon, but still it was no place for a lady.

Alex glanced around. The small cell was empty. All the drunks and vagrants had gone home, leaving only the remnants of their stale odor.

"Hey, Henry, Amelia," the sheriff said as he rose from behind his big desk. "Is this a friendly call?"

"It's business," Alex said. He took off his hat and brushed the hair out of his eyes. Then he held out his hand to the sheriff. "I'm Alex Laird and I brought these two in to get your opinion on a matter of law."

The sheriff looked from them to Alex and took Alex's hand. "Sheriff Picken," he said and pumped hands twice before letting go. "When it comes to law here in Boltonville, I'm it." He looked at Amelia. "What's the problem?"

"Sheriff Picken, this afternoon this man swindled Henry out of my horse."

"Applegate?" The sheriff raised a bushy brow and glanced from Alex to the boy.

"Let me make one thing perfectly clear right now, Ma'am," Alex said. "No one got swindled. If that's what the boy told you then he told you wrong." Alex gave Henry a pointed look. The kid shrugged deeper into his shoulders. "Tell them, kid. Tell them who brought the horse into the game."

"You offered my horse?" Amelia sounded shocked. "Are you telling me that this man didn't trick you into betting Applegate?"

Alex could tell the gal was getting angrier by the minute. Her shoulders went back, her chin went up and she trembled, it appeared. Maybe she wasn't so young after all.

"Well, now, Amelia, you didn't see how fancy his carriage was," Henry said. "Sheriff, he has a brand new racer."

"You bet my horse first?" Amelia interrupted as if she could not believe her brother would do such a thing. Alex believed it. When a man was on a winning streak it was hard not to get caught up in the moment.

"I asked him what it would take to win that carriage and he said . . ."

"I said, the only thing as good as my carriage was that

horse. If I remember right, you said you were willing to bet that horse on your hand." He turned to the gal. "I took him up on it."

"The horse is mine and he didn't have the right to give it away."

"I can verify that," the sheriff said. "The horse is Amelia's dowry. Everybody around here knows it."

"The bet was for the horse."

"He doesn't own the horse," she said as if he were stupid. Alex was far from stupid.

"He shouldn't have bet it."

She stood toe to toe with him. It would have been funny if he weren't such a cynic. He knew the boy was hiding behind his sister. He knew she thought she could involve the sheriff and shame Alex into acting like a gentleman and back out of the bet. She was wrong.

Alex didn't get to be who he was by feeling shame. Bitterness, yes, but never shame.

"What will you take in exchange?"

"I have a new pair of six-shooters," Henry said. There was desperation in his voice.

"The bet was the horse," Alex said.

"I have my late mother's pearl necklace."

"Tell them, Sheriff," he said and crossed his arms over his chest. "I get the horse."

"Let me make sure I'm getting this right," the sheriff said. He eyed Henry sternly. "You were playing cards in the saloon?"

"Yes," Henry mumbled.

"And you bet Applegate against this man's carriage."

"Yes, sir," Henry said. "But I'd been winning all afternoon and I had two pairs, aces high. It was supposed to be a sure thing."

"What did you have?" the sheriff asked Alex.

"I had a royal flush."

The sheriff shook his head. "A bet is a bet, Henry. I've told you and your pa's told you."

"But the horse is mine," Amelia said.

"Well, now by law, that horse belongs to him." The sheriff pointed at Alex.

"You can't just take my property from me," she said.

"Well, now, Amelia, it really ain't your property. He might have been your dowry but he belongs to your father until you get married. If your pa were here, he'd tell you."

Amelia's eyes were wide and she stomped her feet. "That horse belongs to me or my husband."

"The horse belongs to me now," Alex said. "Of course, I could throw your brother in jail and have him horsewhipped instead."

"Can he do that?" Amelia asked the sheriff.

"I'm afraid he can."

"Henry, did you know this?" The boy shrugged. She turned back to Alex her eyes flashing fire and brimstone. "If you take that horse, then you'll have to take me with it."

"If I don't get the horse then I want justice." Alex turned to the sheriff. "Arrest him."

"Sheriff?" Amelia put her hand on the sheriff's arm as if to beg. Alex knew that begging wouldn't make any difference. The law was the law. It was a hard lesson, but one the boy had to learn.

"Now Amelia, how bad do you want Applegate?" the sheriff said. "You need to choose. The horse or the horse-whipping."

The boy finally spoke up. "It's not right, she didn't do anything." He held out his hands. "Arrest me. I'll take the horsewhipping."

"Are you sure?"

"I'm sure."

"It's thirty days and thirty lashes," the sheriff said.

The boy paled visibly. "I'll take it."

Alex hated to lose the horse, but it was good to see the boy taking his salt like a man.

"Wait!" Amelia said. She turned to Alex and put her hand on his chest. He again had a little trouble when she did that. It sent a shock to his heart—which was something, since he didn't really have a heart. "What do you want?" she asked him.

"I want the horse."

"The horse is mine. If you take the horse, then you have to take me."

Alex could tell she meant to scare him. He wasn't scared. Let her come with it. It was no skin off his nose. "Fine."

"Fine."

"Wait!" the sheriff said. "Amelia is a lady born and bred. I can't just let you take her. Now it seems to me that the horse is supposed to be Amelia's dowry, right?"

"Yes," Amelia said.

"And the horse belongs to you, right, Mister?"

"Laird, Alex Laird."

"Then, seems to me, if Amelia expects that horse to be her dowry, and go with her when she gets married, but the horse belongs to you . . . why then . . . I think . . . this whole thing would be solved if you and Amelia . . . get married. Don't you think?" the sheriff said. He seemed pleased with himself for working it all out.

Alex glanced down at the gal. She looked horrified. Her mouth moved open and shut but nothing came out. It was kind of cute, in a strange way.

"I guess that works for me," Alex said just to see what she would do about it.

"We are not married. We aren't even engaged," she said and stamped her foot in frustration.

Alex had to work not to grin, but by golly, he was grinning on the inside. She had worked herself into a lather and he was itching to see how far she would go.

"Well, I think we can take care of the matter right now. Sheriff, do you have a preacher handy?"

"Sure, I happen to know that Reverend Ashley's at the barbershop."

"Then what are we awaiting for?" Alex asked. He took Amelia by the elbow and pulled her out the door. He didn't want to marry her. No siree, he had figured he'd never get married, but it sure was interesting to get her riled up. He figured he'd play out the bluff just to see how far she'd go.

"Now, which way to the barbershop?" Alex asked when they hit the outer walk.

"One block down, second door on the right," the sheriff offered.

"Wait!" Amelia said. "I'm not getting married in a barbershop."

"Well now, darlin', I don't care where it happens as long as it happens. I don't have all day."

They strode down the walk toward the barber's pole. It shone bright white and red as it danced in the afternoon wind. Alex kept a good grip on the gal in case she decided to run off. He wasn't about to let her go anywhere until he got his horse.

"But we can't just get married. We have to get a license and post banns."

He could tell she wanted to stall. "I'm sure the sheriff will give us special dispensation. Won't you, Sheriff?"

The old man was following them with a grin on his face, as if he were responsible for the perfect match. He played right into Alex's hand. "Of course," the sheriff said. "Especially if you're taking Amelia home with you tonight."

"I'm taking the horse," Alex said, "and she claims she's coming."

"Then you'd better be married or her pa will kill me." The old man was now in a hurry. "Henry, get down to the courthouse and have Twyla write you up a license fast."

"But—"

"No buts boy—now git."

"Amelia?"

She glanced at her brother then looked back at Alex. "Get the license."

Alex shook his head. She played hard. Poor thing, she had no idea she was up against the best. Alex turned and stormed into the barbershop. He might not want to get married, but he'd see it through just to call her bluff. He had the upper hand in this case and he was going to keep it.

"I'm looking for Reverend Ashley," he announced as he dragged Amelia into the barbershop. The men inside paused for all of a minute as they took in the sight. Amelia's eyes flashed with fury. The sheriff chuckled and Alex became aware that their little scene had drawn half a dozen or so townspeople out of the shops to see what was going on.

"I'm Reverend Ashley," the preacher said. He stood up from the chair where he'd been playing checkers with an elderly man. "What can I do for you?"

"Amelia would like to be married," Alex said solemnly. "Wouldn't you?" He turned to her.

She narrowed her eyes and he could almost see the imaginary bullets she fired at him. Alex grinned, fueling the fire even further. She took a deep breath and raised her chin, her gaze directly on his face. She dared him. He shook his head. She still didn't get it. He would marry her, just to get his horse. "Yes, Reverend," she said still staring at him. "I want to get married."

That announcement caused a whole lot of commotion in the barbershop. The Reverend raised his hand. "Now, Amelia. Are you sure? I mean, your pa is away. Don't you want to wait?"

"I can wait," Alex said. "Just give me the horse and I'll be on my way."

"The horse is mine," she said under her breath. Then she turned and smiled at the preacher. "We want to be married as soon as possible. In fact Henry ran over to the courthouse to get a license."

"Is that legal?" the Reverend asked the sheriff.

"It's legal," the sheriff said with laughter in his voice. "I'm giving it my blessing."

"Amelia?"

"Now is as good a time as any," she said, "but I would like to be married in the church." She looked at Alex pointedly. He shrugged. He wasn't a church-going man, so church or barbershop didn't make much difference to him.

"Getting married in a church is a serious matter," the Reverend said.

"Business is a serious matter," Alex replied. "This is business."

"Amelia?"

"Let's do it now," she said out loud. Alex swore he heard her finish with, "Before I lose my nerve." The idea made him grin and she reached over and pinched him hard.

"Ow! What was that for?"

"Stop grinning," she ordered.

"Can't a man be happy on his wedding day?"

She shut her mouth and glared at him. He knew in her heart she didn't believe he would do it. But, of course, she didn't know him. If she thought anything other than her own refusal would save her, she was dead wrong.

The men in the barbershop began to come over and introduce themselves to Alex, slapping him on the back. They almost pushed Amelia out of the way, but Alex wasn't having any of that. He didn't want her to get away. Not before he got his horse.

## Chapter Two

The man was a beast. Surely he didn't think they were actually going to get married. He had to be bluffing. After all, he was a card shark and a swindler.

Well, Amelia would play his game. Applegate was her horse. She'd been there when the mare foaled. She'd cleaned off Applegate's nose and watched him take his first steps. She had fallen in love with the animal so quickly that her father had to bribe her to get her out of the barn.

The bribe had been ownership of Applegate. It was what defined her. Amelia intended to marry for love and when she did, she and her lover would take Applegate and found a dynasty of great horses.

Applegate's blood would run through the animals her great grandchildren would breed. It was her destiny. How dare this insufferable man try to bluff her out of it?

She was a shrewd player herself. If she had to, she'd stake her life on the fact that he wouldn't go through with this terrible ruse.

Only one thought kept her going. When she called his bluff, he would fold and refuse to marry her.

16

Then all claims to Applegate would revert back to her. Henry would be safe from punishment, albeit wiser, and she and Applegate would go home and have a nice, calming cup of tea.

"I'm not going to run," she said through gritted teeth and yanked her arm, trying to dislodge his strong grip on her elbow.

"Of course, you're not," he whispered back through his teeth. A forced smile on his face. "You're the one who asked the Reverend to marry us. If you were to run now, I think these men would form a mob and haul you back."

"Don't be ridiculous."

"Ridiculous?" he asked. "Look around."

Amelia did look around and swallowed a jolt of panic. The men in the barbershop were so happy, you'd think she was a pariah and that they couldn't wait to be rid of her.

The sheriff had been no help at all. In fact he had a twinkle in his eye that showed how proud of himself he was for setting up the whole thing. Of course, Mr. Laird didn't know it but the sheriff was fond of bets and betting. Amelia's guess was that he had a side bet going on who would back out first.

She wouldn't. Her whole life depended on it.

"I'll go get the ladies," Mr. Pimly hollered. "I'm certain my wife would love to see a wedding."

"Shall I contact the Ladies' Brigade?" the barber asked.

"I hardly think that's necessary," Amelia demurred.

"Seems to me they still got that wedding dress they made for your sister. I'm sure they'll be happy to pull it out of the tissue for you."

"Wedding dress?" the gambler asked.

Amelia turned her gaze on him and dared him with a lifted eyebrow. "Why not? This is my wedding after all. I think I'd prefer not to get married in a riding outfit. Thank you,

Mr. Holster, it would be lovely if the ladies want to let me borrow the dress."

"Of course, I'll need a few moments to change," Amelia said. Enough time to make the man sweat, and perhaps the sight of an actual wedding gown would help Mr. Laird change his mind.

There was a flash of something in his eyes just before his expression turned dull. "As long as it doesn't take too long. I would like to get home by nightfall." His tone was dismissive and arrogant.

She wanted to belt him. "I can assure you it will take as long as it takes."

It was then that Henry came rushing in, out of breath, waving a piece of paper. "I got the license."

"Good," the insufferable Alex Laird said and grabbed it. He glanced over the writing. "Looks like everything is in order. Let's get to the church."

"I want to wait for the wedding dress," she said when he pulled her forward.

"Why are you stalling?"

"I am not stalling," she said and raised her chin.

"Are you having second thoughts? Because it won't be pretty when you tell these fellas and their womenfolk that you changed your mind."

"I'm not changing my mind," she said, her voice rising with frustration. She really wanted to hurt this man. In fact, when Papa came back she would enjoy watching him ride after him with a shotgun full of buckshot.

She planted her feet so hard that he had to quit tugging or he'd drag her. Surely, he wouldn't drag her through the streets. "Why are you in such a hurry? Are you getting cold feet?"

"My feet are just fine."

"Then you can wait for a wedding dress to be pulled out of the tissue," she said and remained firm. "And no, you cannot go with me while I get dressed. You'll simply have to trust that I will not run away."

The men overheard her and laughed. Someone in the back made a ribald comment about the gambler's hurry. Amelia flushed with embarrassment but Alex Laird didn't seem upset by it at all. Instead he stood toe to toe with her and lifted his mouth in a sexy-as-heck grin and simply looked at her. His look touched her face, and her mouth then dipped lower. "Why can't I go with you? I'm handy with buttons."

"Really!" Amelia took a step back and tried not to blush. The whole thing was ridiculous. This man was no gentleman. Why, he looked at her as if she were something he thought about buying and couldn't wait to get home. How dare he?

She narrowed her eyes and trembled with anger. "You are going to have to trust that I am old enough to dress myself."

"Henry," Alex said, his gaze returning to Amelia's and holding it. She thought she read a challenge in it. As if he expected her to trick him.

"Yes, Sir?"

"Go get the horse."

"I beg your pardon?" she and Henry said at the same time.

"Get the horse," he said and slowly, deliberately looked from her to Henry. "If your sister is going to be out of my sight, then I want the horse within my sight."

Amelia gasped in outrage. "Do you think that I would run away and take my horse?"

"He's my horse and, honey, you don't look like the kind who'd run." He looked at her again. "But I'm the kind of man who hedges his bets." He turned back to Henry. "Now, get the horse."

Henry glanced at Amelia.

"Go!" Alex commanded and Henry sent his sister a look of apology just before he ducked out the door. She was going to have a long talk with that boy when this was over.

"There's a mob of ladies comin' down the sidewalk," Homer Cuzin declared from the doorway. "Looks like they got the dress in hand."

Alex tilted his head at her. "After you." He swished his hand in a courtly manner indicating the door. Amelia waited a long moment while she contemplated how much trouble she'd be in if she kicked the man in the shin.

The look on his face told her he'd be happy to see her try. Well, she wouldn't give him the satisfaction.

Instead she picked up her skirts, stuck her nose in the air and stomped outside. The sunlight had cooled in the afternoon. There was a slight chill in the air that warned of an unexpected cold snap. Amelia smelled frost. She thought it best to match her mood to the weather. Yes, a frosty demeanor might serve her well except that she couldn't get past the anger that Alex Laird stirred in her.

The man was intolerable.

"Yoo-hoo, Amelia!" Mrs. Selis shouted with obvious delight. "Amelia Morgan, what is this we hear that you are getting married this very afternoon? Why so sudden? Why ever didn't we know you were engaged?"

Amelia bit her lip and took in the group of curious stares that surrounded Mrs. Selis. It seemed that all of the women in Boltonville had converged in the middle of Main Street. The whole town seemed to hold its breath. Even the wagons had slowed to hear her reply.

"Yes, I'm getting married," Amelia said, "permanently, as in for the rest of our lives. Right, dear?" She grabbed Alex and pushed him into the center of the group. "Everyone, this is Alex Laird. Alex is my fiancé and he wants to get married straight away."

"Why Mr. Laird, how lovely to meet you. I'm Blanche Selis, and with me is the Boltonville Ladies' Brigade."

"How do you do," Alex said and took Mrs. Selis' outstretched hand. He bent over and gave her fingers a kiss, charm oozing out of him. Amelia narrowed her eyes. "I'm surprised to see so much interest in Amelia," he said.

She wanted to kick him. What did he think? That no one cared about her? "Of course they are interested," Amelia said, taking hold of his arm. "I'm no bumpkin."

"Ever since her mama died so many years ago, we ladies have made it our business to see that the Morgan girls had the proper upbringing their mama would have wanted for them," Mrs. Selis said with a smile. "It's only natural that we care when one of our girls is contemplating a hurried wedding." She glanced over at Amelia. "Especially when her papa is out of town and we are only just now meeting her fiancé. There wouldn't be a particular reason you are in this rush, now would there?"

"Mrs. Selis!" Amelia blushed. "How could you ask that?"

"Just checking, dear, after all your sister was a bit loo—"

"My sister acted on a mission of mercy," Amelia reminded her. "Besides they are happily married now."

"Well, I was simply letting you know that if you are in some kind of trouble, you can tell us. We're here to help."

"Yes, Amelia, do tell if there is something I should know about." The despicable man turned to her with a grin.

"There is nothing for you to know," she said loud enough for everyone to hear. Then between her teeth she added, "And you darn well know it."

"Do I?" He raised an eyebrow at her. Finally he let her off the hook and turned back to the ladies. "I'm sorry for the hurry ladies but, you see, Amelia is so enamored that she declared she was going home with me tonight. I thought a wedding beforehand was in order."

"Ah!" Amelia gasped, shocked at what he insinuated. "I did not."

"No?"

She closed her mouth and narrowed her eyes. He responded with a cool smile. She turned her back on him and came face to face with the interested mob. "I—"

"It's all right, dear," Mrs. Selis said and patted her. "We understand. He is a very handsome man." The older woman looked Mr. Laird up and down. "We were young once, too, weren't we ladies?"

The crowd twittered in what Amelia could only interpret as anticipation.

"Now, dear, surely you don't want to get married in that old frock."

"We have the wedding dress we made for your sister," Mrs. Lance offered. She smiled cheerfully and held up the gown. "Isn't it lovely that the dress is getting so much use this year? What with Madeline marrying just a few months ago and all."

"Why look, Henry's brought you your pet horse to ride," Mrs. Selis said. "How sweet is that? He even put your best saddle on it."

"Yes," Amelia muttered. "My little brother is a saint, isn't he?"

"Come on, let's take you over to the millinery and get you changed."

Amelia glanced over at Alex who took Applegate's reins from Henry and stroked *her* horse's neck. "Go ahead, sweetheart," Alex said. "Applegate and I will be waiting for you at the church."

"Henry will see that you are." She glared daggers at her brother just before the ladies pulled her off.

"Oh, don't worry," Alex said with a sly grin. "I wouldn't miss our wedding for the world . . . sweetheart."

Amelia wanted to throw something at him, but it would be unseemly. Especially with the entire Boltonville Ladies' Brigade watching.

The church was packed with townspeople. Alex found the whole situation fascinating. It seemed the men were happy to have Amelia married because she had a younger sister who was purported to be stunning. Rumor was that Amelia's father had said the younger could not wed until Amelia and her older sister were married.

The ladies, on the other hand, simply loved a wedding. In fact the barber told him they were all hopeless romantics and had made the wedding gown for Amelia's older sister. The story was that the ladies worked hard to get the two girls married, but Amelia had never been interested in any of the men. The town had almost given up hope for her.

He might ask Amelia why she had never been interested, but the truth was he really didn't care. This wasn't about the girl. It was about the horse.

He moved to the front of the church to stand next to the preacher. Henry stood beside Alex and shifted nervously from one foot to the other.

"Your sister will be fine," Alex assured him. "I'm not forcing her to do this. All she has to do is give me the horse and I'll be on my way."

"You don't understand," Henry said with a shake of his head. "Amelia is wicked stubborn. Now the whole town is here and when you jilt her, it's going to look very bad for her."

"I'm not going to jilt her."

"I know you're a good card player and all," Henry said, "a fine bluffer, but mister you don't know my sister. She's got a great mind for cards and she knows you're bluffing. I swear. I've never been able to beat her."

"Your sister plays cards?"

"Only at home," Henry said. "But watch out, she's the best I've ever seen."

"So what are you saying?"

"I'm saying that if you don't want to get married right now, you'd better be heading for the back door, because she's going to call your bluff."

"I'm not leaving without the horse." It suddenly got very still inside the church. Alex looked up to see why. Amelia stepped into the center aisle and he caught his breath.

It was as if someone had kicked him in the stomach. She stepped toward him in a beaded and embroidered white gown and suddenly a fierce possessiveness washed over him. This woman, this beauty, was his for the taking.

His hands shook as he helped her up the small step to the altar. Her auburn hair was twisted up away from her face framing it like fiery chocolate silk. White lace covered her face, accenting the deep blue of her eyes. She smelled of flowers and a womanly scent warm and soft.

He kept his hand on her elbow, afraid she'd run away. She tilted her head and looked at him with curiosity. Her lush mouth parted, her lips moist. He leaned toward her and lifted the veil away from her face.

"What are you doing?" she whispered.

"I want to see my bride."

"Look, you don't have to do this," she continued in a low voice. "Papa has specialized in good breeding stock. When he gets back I'm sure he'll be happy to compensate you."

Alex felt as if his brain was frozen on just one thought.

This stunning creature was about to become his wife. That would make her his. "I want Applegate," he said, but it was no longer just the horse he wanted.

"You'll have to marry me to get him."

"That's what I'm doing." He liked the frustration he saw flit through her eyes. It was there for only a moment, then it was gone.

"Fine."

"Fine," Alex said and turned toward the preacher.

"Dearly beloved," the preacher began. "We are gathered here this afternoon to join this man and this woman in Holy Matrimony. Marriage is an important step. It is a step in which a woman entrusts a man with her life and the lives of their future children. It is not to be taken lightly or with haste."

The preacher stopped and gave Alex a hard look, but he refused to back down. For some reason he couldn't explain, he suddenly wanted this ceremony more than anything he'd wanted in a long time, if only to say that once in his life, a beautiful woman stood beside him and pledged her troth. It would be a memory to warm him on a lonely night.

"If there is anyone here who knows any reason why these two should not be joined, speak now or forever hold your peace."

There was silence. Someone coughed in the background. Henry shuffled and Alex turned to look at the boy. He opened his mouth as if to speak, but Alex glared him down. Henry shook his head.

"Then let us begin," the preacher said when the challenge was not raised. "Do you, Alex Laird, take Miss Amelia Morgan as your lawfully wedded wife to have and to hold, to love and to cherish, for richer or poorer in sickness and in health for as long as you both shall live?"

"I do."

"Do you, Amelia Morgan, take this man, Alex Laird, as

your lawfully wedded husband to have and to hold, to love and to obey, for richer or poorer, in sickness and in health for as long as you both shall live?"

"I will do everything but obey," she challenged. The crowd in the church gasped.

Alex raised an eyebrow at her defiant look, raised her gloved hand and kissed it. "Don't worry," he told the crowd. "I enjoy a good challenge."

The church erupted in good-hearted laughter. Amelia's face flushed a lovely shade of pink, but her gaze was mutinous. Alex leaned toward her. "Last chance to back out."

"Never," she hissed.

"Fine."

"Fine," she echoed.

"What God has joined together, let no man tear asunder," the preacher declared. "You may now kiss the bride."

Kissing this spitfire was exactly what Alex had in mind. He put his hands on her waist and pulled her toward him. Her lips were soft and parted in shock. Apparently she hadn't thought as far as the kissing. Her shock encouraged him.

She tasted sweet like candy and innocence. Her hands trembled as she clutched his lapels. Alex wondered briefly if she'd ever been kissed.

He eased her into the intimacy of it, drawing her hard against him. He explored her lips. His tongue touching the dip where they parted. She sighed and leaned into him. Her surrender was so sweet, he wanted nothing more than to take her away and make her his.

For now, the surrender was enough he thought, and pulled away. After all, they were in a church with an entire town looking on.

"Ladies and gentlemen of Boltonville, may I present to you, Mr. and Mrs. Alex Laird."

Alex glanced down at Amelia. She still had her eyes

closed as if uncertain what to do next. He kissed her cheek and squeezed her. "Come on, Wife. Let's get going. We have a long way home."

Her eyes popped open, slightly glazed from the kiss.

"Oh," she said when she realized what had happened. He had kissed her and she had buckled. The very thought made him want to laugh out loud with joy. It might be interesting to have a wife.

"Going home?"

"Yes, we've got a two-hour ride ahead of us and it's nearly dark."

"I have to change," she said vaguely. "The dress belongs to the ladies."

"You'd better get going then," he replied and looked at his pocket watch. "Applegate and I are leaving in five minutes. Of course, you're welcome to stay here . . ."

"I'll be ready," she said, the glint returning to her eye. She lifted her skirt and pushed through the well-wishing crowd. Someone called for her to toss the bouquet of hastily-gathered fall flowers that had been pressed into her hands when she entered the church. She paused briefly, flung the flowers over her shoulder and kept moving.

Alex nodded. He liked efficiency in a woman. He had thought he'd never marry, but this afternoon fate in the form of a daring boy had stepped in. Now he was married to a spitfire.

It wouldn't last, of course. When her father found out there'd be a reckoning, but for the first time in years he felt alive. This was a new game with rules he had yet to learn. It would make life interesting . . . while it lasted.

He had kissed her.

And she had liked it. She touched her lips as she hurried off to the millinery to change back into her riding clothes.

Even worse, he had actually married her. She glanced at the thin gold band on her finger. He'd worn it on his pinky. It had a small diamond chip and she wondered if it had any significance to him.

She was now officially Mrs. Alex Laird. The thought made her heart pound against her chest. Papa was going to kill her. Right now she wished Maddie and Beth were in town. She was in desperate need of sister talk.

"Amelia! What are you doing here?" Mrs. Otis, the milliner, said when Amelia rushed into the shop. "I thought you were going to get married."

"I did get married," Amelia said and unbuttoned as many of the buttons on the back of the dress as she could reach while she scurried over to her riding clothes. "Now my husband is in a hurry to leave and if I'm not dressed in time, he'll take Applegate and go off without me!"

Mrs. Otis shook her head and tugged the curtain around the dressing area, closing them off. "Honey child, that man is not going to leave you. He was just trying to put the fear of God in you is all. It's perfectly natural for a man to want to control his wife. He figures he'll make a stand right off."

Amelia squirmed out of the dress as far as she could. "No, this man really means it. He will leave me."

"Why would he leave you? He just married you. The last thing he's going to do is to go off and leave a pretty thing like you."

"Right now, I'm not willing to take that chance." Amelia stepped out of the gown and handed it to Mrs. Otis. "Please thank the ladies for being so kind as to let me wear this dress. It would have been sad to be married in my riding outfit."

She tugged on her blouse and flung her riding skirt over her head, wiggling it down over her petticoats. She did up the three buttons at the waist and stepped out of the silk slippers Mrs. Selis had loaned her.

Stomping her feet into her riding boots, she was glad she had never liked the button kind. She doubted Alex Laird would allow her the time to button them up. Amelia tugged the curtain aside and looked out the window to see her new husband climbing into his racer. Applegate was already tied to the back of the carriage.

"Shoot, shoot, shoot," Amelia muttered under her breath. She grabbed her gloves and hat and ran out the door.

"Bye, dear," Mrs. Otis called. Amelia gave a wave behind her and watched as the cursed man started down the street with her horse in tow. He was actually going to make her chase after him in front of the whole town. Fine. She would show him that she was not that easily put off.

Swallowing the humiliation, she picked up her skirts and ran after him. Alex Laird was not going to get away with Applegate. She thought he had learned that when she said, "I do."

"Hey, Laird," one of the men called. "You forgot something!"

"No, I don't think so," he had the gall to reply and kept going.

Amelia cursed him for his sorry heart and broke into an all-out sprint. She caught up to the wagon to the cheers and laughter of the crowd. Grabbing the edge she hopped up into the seat. "You forgot me," she said, trying not to sound as if she were dying for breath—which she was, due to her darn corset.

"Oh, I didn't forget you," Alex said.

She glanced at him. There was a strange warmth in his voice. His dark eyes were serious, but his mouth had the tilt of a smile. He was laughing at her.

"All you had to do was holler," he said. "I would have stopped."

"I am a lady, not a washerwoman," she said indignantly,

straightening her skirts. "I do not *holler*." She plopped her hat on her head and tugged on her gloves.

"Well, that's good to know," he said and gave the reins a snap. The horse in front of the carriage was sleek and happy to break out into a run.

"Show off," she muttered and clung to her hat with one hand and the side of the racer with the other.

He laughed out loud and raced them down the road. The town of Boltonville disappeared behind a hill and Amelia wondered if she would ever call it home again.

## Chapter Three

Supper time came and went. Still he didn't stop. At least he'd slowed the horse down to a solid trot after galloping the first few miles.

Amelia took in the rolling countryside. The long patches of thick woods with small fields carved out Wisconsin was a place of beauty.

They headed east. Amelia knew that Lake Michigan was east of Boltonville, but she hadn't seen it since she was a small child. Perhaps he lived near the lake or maybe they were headed toward Chicago. She eyed Alex Laird. He dressed the part of a slick gambler. She wondered if he even had a barn for Applegate. Goodness, she knew nothing about the man.

She turned and edged into the corner of her seat to get a good look at her husband. He was as tall as her brother Robert, with shoulders as wide as her other brother Griffin's. His hands were square and held the reins with confidence.

She liked that he didn't hurt the horse's mouth by holding the reins too tightly and he never used the whip that sat so

stylishly beside his long legs. It was clear he was as confident around horses as he was with cards.

"What?" he asked, catching her staring.

"I was wondering where we were going," she said.

"Why does it matter?" he asked. "You made it quite clear
that all you cared about was your horse."

It struck her suddenly that he might have meant to sell off
Applegate immediately. That would be one way to get rid of
her. "I wonder if you have a barn for Applegate, because if
you mean only to sell him, my brother Robert would pay you
handsomely."

"Your brother Robert."

"He is older than Henry by seven years," she said. "He has
the cash."

"Where was he when we were getting married?"

"He's in Wyoming."

"Wyoming as in the territory?"

"Yes."

There was a long pause. "I don't intend to sell the horse."

"Oh . . . Good." She faced front and clasped her hands in
her lap. An icy wind rushed by, lifting the edges of her wool
skirt. She tucked it closer to her legs.

"Are you having doubts?" he asked. "It's a bit late for that
isn't it . . . wife?"

"What do you mean by doubts?"

"Has it just now occurred to you that I am a gambler and
may be without a home?"

"I don't care if you have a home," she said and crossed
her arms over her chest. The temperature felt as if it was
dropping by the minute. "I do care if you have a barn.
Applegate is too beautiful to be left out in the wild. He
should have a warm stall and a nice bag of oats."

"So, you don't care if you have to sleep on the ground as
long as the horse has a barn."

"I've slept on the floor before," she said, tamping down her sudden panic. Was the man she had just married penniless? She glanced at the fine carriage they rode in. Surely not. A shiver went through her.

"Princess, you don't look as if you've ever slept anywhere but on a stack of mattresses the Queen of England herself would envy."

"I've made do in the past."

He snorted in disbelief.

"I have," she said. "Papa took us camping for a whole week last year."

"Camping." He shook his head. "It figures."

"What's wrong with camping? Fresh air is very healthful." She wiggled, trying to get some feeling back into her toes.

"Only a spoiled princess would think so," he said. "It's a different story if you *have* to sleep under the stars when the wind blows cold out of the north and a blanket of snow falls."

"I can sleep wherever I have to as long as Applegate is taken care of," she said bravely. Her thoughts were not so brave. She huddled into her jacket and tried not to imagine what it would be like to have to sleep in an alley.

"Don't worry," he said, finally breaking the silence that had allowed her thoughts to grow more and more wild. "I take care of what is mine."

Her stomach rumbled loudly and he laughed. "From the sound of it, it's a good thing I do. You haven't made it four hours and your stomach is protesting that it's hungry. What if I were a vagabond, hmm?"

"I have a few coins and my saddle," she said evenly and lifted her chin. "I will make do."

He reached under the seat and pulled out a thick woolen blanket. "Here, you're freezing. We're about an hour from

Applegate's warm barn. Wrap up. You don't want to catch pneumonia and die. Then Applegate really would be all mine."

She gave him a look and huddled into the blanket. She was immediately warmer. She glanced at him, still dressed in a fine suit with a waistcoat, but no overcoat. "Are you cold?" she asked. "There's enough blanket for both of us."

"Seems to me that to share the blanket, you'll have to sit closer to me," he said and pointed out the wide gap between them on the seat. "Are you sure you want to do that?"

"Are you implying that I'm afraid of you?" She scooted next to him. "Because that would be absurd. I married you, didn't I?"

She tucked the blanket in around them, clasped her hands in her lap and ignored the heat of his gaze.

"Yes," he said. "You married me, and quite nicely too."

"What do you mean by that?"

"I mean that, for a stubborn bride, you looked lovely." He reached over and stroked her cheek. The cool leather of his glove belayed the warmth he felt inside, but it was a gentle touch, one that made her wonder.

She flushed under his gaze. "Thank you, I think."

"Lovely," he said and dropped his hand, his eyes returning to the dark road. "But foolish."

Her back stiffened. "I realize that you don't know me but you will find that I am far from a fool."

"Really?"

"Yes."

"Then why did you marry a man you'd just met? You know nothing about me except that I am better at card games than your precious baby brother. Any grown woman with a lick of sense would have known better."

"I know you are a stubborn man," she said and wiggled as far away from him as she could while still keeping the blanket. "Are you saying it is foolish to marry a stubborn man? If that were the case then no woman would ever marry."

He laughed. "Little fool, what if I am dirt poor? What will you do? Go running back to your papa?"

"And leave you with Applegate? I think not."

He sobered. "Do you care only for the fine animal?"

"Applegate is my life," she said. "I would be nothing without him. Although, I must admit that I will miss my books."

"So you are an educated woman."

"I like to read."

"No doubt fairy tales from the Brothers Grimm."

"What is wrong with fairy tales? They have merit. There's a moral to each and every one. Why even the First Lady reads them, or so I've heard."

He laughed heartily. "I suppose you are an expert on politics, too."

She blushed. "I read the papers."

"How old are you Amelia?"

"A woman never tells her age."

"How old?" he insisted.

"I'm within marrying age."

"Amelia—"

"All right, I'm twenty if you must know."

He seemed to relax. He had been afraid she was either too young or a spinster. She bit her lip and tried not to think about her spinsterhood. "How old are you?"

She guessed he was about Robert's age or maybe a little older.

"I'll be thirty in a few months."

"Have you never married?"

"No."

"Why not?" she pressed. Was there something wrong with him? It was a little late now if there was.

"Never felt the need," he said and shot her a sideways glance. "I'm not the family kind."

"I see."

"And you?"

She settled back against the cushioned seat. "I guess you have never been in love."

"What has love got to do with marriage?"

"Why love and marriage go hand in hand. You can't have one without the other."

"You do read too many fairy tales. We're married and we are not in love."

"Not yet."

"Ah, a romantic."

"What's wrong with romance?"

"Nothing, I suppose, if you like to keep your head in the clouds and horse blinders on."

"I am not blind."

"No, just stubborn, fool-headed and naive." He shook his head. "Did you even think before you said 'I do?' What if I'm a drunk?"

"You are not."

"How would you know?"

"You're nose isn't red and your eyes are far from blood-shot."

"That doesn't mean I might not drink myself to sleep every night. What if I have a terrible temper? What if I tend to take it out on those around me?"

"You wouldn't dare hurt me."

He leaned down until his nose practically touched hers. "I'm your husband now. I can dare to do whatever I choose with you."

The threat in his words was not lost on her. She tried not to think about the marriage bed or anything else that was yet to come.

He sat back up, dismissing her. "By law, I own you now. Just like I own Applegate. You should know that there are men out there who would treat that horse much better than any woman they own. Especially a fool-headed woman."

"You promised to love and to cherish," she pointed out. "You promised in a church before God and witnesses."

"What if I don't believe in God? What if I just did those things so that I could take the horse that was by rights mine?"

"You believe in God."

"What if I don't?"

"You do," she insisted. "Anyone with a brain does."

"Anyone with a brain wouldn't run off and marry a complete and total stranger."

Her stomach rumbled loudly again. He glanced at her. "Don't worry there will be food at the end of this little journey."

"I'm not worried," she said. "I don't care if I eat or not as long as Applegate is taken care of."

"Applegate isn't your worry any more," he said. "The animal is mine and I take care of what is mine."

She closed her mouth to keep from correcting him and slumped into the blanket. Technically he was right. Applegate was his and so was she, but only because of antiquated opinions regarding women's inferiority. Maybe she should join the suffragettes. She could march on Washington and demand that women have a voice. She glanced at the man beside her and knew he would be more than happy to let her go.

Even better, she could stay with her horse and do her best to change opinions one man at a time, starting with Mr. Alex Laird.

Amelia woke with a start when the carriage came to a halt. She sat up when she realized that she had been leaning against her husband. She checked her mouth. Thank goodness, she hadn't drooled. What would the man think of her then?

"Where are we?" she asked and looked around. They had turned off the road and up to a wide gate. It was made of wrought iron, twisted to keep intruders out, or something in. "Mr. Laird?"

He stood next to the gate and lit a lantern. Then he pulled out the key to the padlock that held the chain around the gate. "This is home," he said simply.

The lantern threw shadows that bounced ominously off the gate and she pulled the blanket close. This was going to be her new home and she refused to be afraid. The wind whipped up, cutting through the trees, shaking loose the leaves remaining after the first frost.

Alex took the reins and pulled the racer through the gate, then stopped and relocked it behind them. The light shone on a drive that ran ahead through the trees. Curious, Amelia huddled under the blankets but looked about, hoping for a glimpse of her new home. She saw nothing but dark, cold woods. The fence disappeared into the shadows revealing nothing of its length or breadth.

Applegate let out a whoosh which startled her. She glanced back at her horse. "It's okay, boy," she murmured. "This is our new home. I'm sure we'll get used to it."

Alex climbed back up and snapped the reins. They followed a long and winding path through the trees. It sloped up and, in the distance, Amelia could hear the sound of waves crashing. The scent of water filled the air and she realized they were very near the lake.

The path opened up at the crest of the hill. There was a wide circular drive paved in stone. A dark fountain larger than anything Amelia had seen before stood in the center.

Beyond the drive was a massive house. It was two stories built in the federal style. "A brick house?"

"Yes."

She studied it while Alex came around and helped her down from the carriage. "And this is your home?" The words came out in a whisper. The house was the biggest she had ever seen in her entire life and considering her father's wealth, that was saying something.

Alex only glanced at the twin oak doors. "I keep my things here." He untied Applegate and, taking hold of the reins, moved him around to the right side of the house.

Amelia followed. She didn't know where to look first, at the house or where Alex was going. He acted as if the house was not important. She decided she would look less naive if she didn't stare at it, no matter how much she wanted to. There would be plenty of time to see it all later. After all, she was married to Alex and that meant she was now a part of this place.

The wind howled wickedly as she turned a corner. The path eased down the edge of a cliff to a large low-slung barn made of stone. Alex opened the big wooden door and Amelia went in behind Applegate and him.

The barn was squat, but very long with twelve stalls. It was warm and smelled of sweet hay and animals. Alex hung the lantern on the second stall and opened the gate. Amelia noticed that the stall was clean, the air relatively fresh. Applegate nodded as if in approval.

Alex led the horse in, turned him, then lowered the gate, leaving the stallion room to push out his head and take a good look around. The other horses sniffed the air and snorted.

Amelia stroked Applegate's fine nose. "It's okay, boy. This is a very nice home."

When Alex returned with the other horse, he placed it in

a stall farther down, and then took off his coat and hung it from a nail. He picked up a bucket and filled it with fresh water. He emptied it in the water trough inside Applegate's stall. The animal sniffed the water then drank while Alex did the same for the other horse.

"How many horses do you own?" Amelia asked.

"A few," Alex said as he split a fresh bale of hay. He spread it inside the stallion's stall. Then he opened a barrel and scooped out a measure of oats. The oats went into the feed trough.

Amelia watched him work and felt a measure of guilt. She looked around, found a curry brush, and brushed down Applegate while Alex worked on the other horse. It improved her spirits to see that her baby would be well cared for. She finished her chore and let Applegate get to his dinner. Alex opened the stall gate for her. "I've never seen a barn so grand."

"The previous owner loved horses," Alex said with a shrug. "He had an architect from Chicago come and design the barn." Alex lifted up the lantern. "See how the center is paved with cobblestone? The two troughs on either side carry away waste so that the barn is easy to clean and stays fresh. The low roof keeps in the heat during the winter and the vents along the top open up to keep the temperature cooler in summer."

She glanced at the row of stalls and counted at least five curious animals with their heads out. "It must take quite a staff to maintain the place. Why did no one come and help you with the racer?"

"The Strasburgs watch over the place for me," he said and grabbed his coat. "They are good at doing what I ask, but they are rather old. I told them not to bother with the place at night. Anything that happens after dark I can take care of."

"That's very thoughtful of you," she said and followed him outside. The wind buffeted her as she stepped out the door.

"Not thoughtful," he said and caught her by the waist. "Necessary." The wind had churned up so much that if Alex hadn't taken hold of her, she might have been blown right off the cliff.

Amelia glanced at the house looming above the stable. Truth be told she preferred to be close to Applegate. She wondered if Alex would allow her to stay in the barn. Her heart pounded at the thought of being alone at night with this stranger who was now her husband.

"Come on," he said. "Let's get you inside." He had to shout next to her ear to be heard above the wind. He pulled her to the large doors, pulled a key out of his breast pocket and unlocked one.

The wind pushed her inside and she turned in the darkness as he pulled the door closed. The sound echoed through the foyer.

"Just a moment and I'll get a lamp lit."

She waited, hugging her waist and trying not to be spooked by the darkness, the echoing noises and the nearness of the man to whom she had given her life. There was the scrape of a match against a hard surface and the flame burst to life, illuminating the small space around her. Alex quickly took the chimney off a lamp and lit it. The sharp scent of kerosene filled the air. He trimmed the wick, blew out the match and replaced the chimney. Then he turned to her. "Let's go into the kitchen and see what there is to eat."

Amelia glanced around. The foyer was full of boxes. There were things piled in floor-to-ceiling mounds. Wooden boxes and barrels and what looked like a stuffed moose head. She picked her way behind him as he walked down a thin path that led into the room on the left. It was once a parlor but now it too was filled nearly to the ceiling.

The furniture was covered in dust cloths and surrounded by tables and chairs and a hat rack and coat racks. Alex couldn't have used the fireplace if he'd wanted to. It was completely blocked.

She followed Alex through a second parlor into a dining room the size of her sister's entire house. Everywhere there were stacks head high, sometimes higher. It amazed her. She had to admit to being more than a little curious as to what it all was.

"Wow," she said. "Are these all your things?"

"I'm a collector."

"Right."

They made their way through a butler's pantry and into a large kitchen. In comparison to the rest of the house, the kitchen was surprisingly clean. A fire was banked in the walk-in fireplace. A simmering teapot hung from a hook to the side of the fire. In the center of the room sat a simple oak table and four chairs.

The floor was wood plank and freshly swept. A pot of something sat on the back of a black stove. It smelled of wonderfully rich gravy, vegetables and beef. Amelia's stomach growled at the fragrance. "Smells wonderful."

"Mrs. Strasburg laid claim to the kitchen years ago. Since she is a great cook I give her free rein." He set the lamp on the table. "Go on, see for yourself." He gestured toward the stove, then leaned against the table and folded his arms across his chest.

Grabbing a towel, Amelia lifted the lid to the pot to see a fine roast nestled in gravy. Potatoes and carrots sat beside it. The meal was kept warm by the low bank of coals beneath it.

"Does she always leave food on the stove?"

"When she knows I'll be returning. There's a loaf of bread in the cupboard."

"Wonderful," Amelia said. "Shall we eat?"

"Help yourself."

She washed her hands in the spotless sink, wiped them on a towel and turned to him. "Where do you keep your dishes?"

"Have a look around," he said, his eyes dark and unreadable. "The cupboards are full."

Amelia indulged her curiosity. She searched the floor-to-ceiling cupboards and found plates, goblets, teacups, and pots and pans of all varieties. There were drawers full of sugar and coffee and flour, and three drawers full of silverware. She picked up a spoon.

"Yes, it's real silver," he said.

Embarrassed that he caught her assessing, she reached back in and picked out two full place settings. "I was thinking only of setting the table," she fibbed. "My mother always said a pretty table makes the meal better."

He didn't say anything as she pulled out dishes and placed them on the table beside him. Once it was set, she put the pot roast on a serving platter and placed it on the table. "What about butter for the bread?"

"There," he said and pointed toward a door. She opened it and discovered a pantry that smelled of spices. A whole section of the pantry was devoted to cheese in various wrappings. Hams hung from the ceiling. Piles of apples and potatoes spilled out of bins. Beside the bins was an ornate cabinet. She opened it to find the inside covered in tin. A large block of ice sat behind a pitcher of milk and a beautiful silver butter plate.

"It's an icebox."

Amelia nearly jumped out of her skin at the sound of Alex's voice. She straightened and looked at him. He rested against the doorjamb, watching her. "I know that," she said and retrieved the butter. "My Aunt Silvia has one." She pulled out the butter and turned toward the door.

"See, now that's the difference between you and me," he said.

"What?"

"I had never seen one before I won it off a peddler. Now Strasburg has to go to the ice house every couple of weeks and bring home fresh ice." He straightened and pushed away from the door. "Not so often in the winter of course."

"Of course." Amelia shook her head. She knew her family was considered well off, but she had never seen so much food in her life. It was as if she had stepped into an enchanted kitchen. All she had to do was wish and the food would be there. She shook her head at the rows of canned peaches and pears. Henry would die happy if he could see this pantry. Something her brothers had taught her was that young men ate twice their weight in food. It could be that Alex did too.

She stepped out of the cupboard to find Alex watching her.

"So, what do you think?"

"That pantry is overwhelming."

"Mrs. Strasburg," he said as explanation and shrugged. "This is the only part of the house I let her take care of."

"Why?" Amelia asked as she set the butter down on the table.

"The rest is for my things. She doesn't need to be poking around in it . . . and neither do you."

"I see." She folded her hands in front of her and waited. "What?"

"Aren't you going to wash your hands before we eat?"

"Right." He turned and moved to the sink. She watched as he rolled up the sleeves of his shirt, revealing strong forearms. There was something about a man with strength in his arms that gave her a slight shiver. She tore her gaze away from him and turned it to the table.

"I have to say I've never seen so many things in my life."

"My estate is large," he said and wiped his hands on a towel. "So your fears of sleeping in an alley should be gone."

She blinked. "My fears? How did you?"

"I saw the look of horror on your face earlier when you asked me if I had a home to go to. I figure it must have hit you that I was a gambler and gamblers don't usually have homes."

"Some gamblers do," she said. "You obviously do."

"Yes, but you didn't know that," he said and held out a chair for her.

She sat down and he tucked her and the chair into the table as if she were as light as a feather. "For all you knew I was penniless except for the racer and Applegate."

"I knew you weren't homeless," she argued and waited for him to sit down. He sat and placed his napkin in his lap.

"Exactly how did you know?" he asked. He put his elbows on the table and studied her.

"I've seen many a homeless man since the war. You, sir, are too clean to be homeless."

"I could have bought a bath at the bathhouse."

"It's more than that," she said stubbornly. "You have an air of wealth about you. Which is why I could not believe that you wouldn't give Applegate back to me. I mean, it is pretty clear you don't need him." She waved her hand about.

Alex laughed at her. "Silly gal," he said and hooked his finger under her chin. "Things are not what they seem. I have been homeless many times and I suspect I probably will be again. What you see around you is merely a run of good luck. When that luck changes—and it will—I'm going to need everything I have to make it through the bad times."

His fingers were warm on her chin. He caressed her cheek

with the back of his hand, ran his forefinger along her lips. His touch left a tingling trail that went clear to her belly. "You've hitched your wagon to a gambler's star," he said softly. "Enjoy the good times while you can, for they never last."

## Chapter Four

"It seems to me that you are the one afraid of being penniless and living in alleys." Amelia put down her fork and leveled her gaze at him.

He sat up straight, startled by her observation. "I've been hungry before," he said. "I survived it. Why would I be afraid?"

"Why else would you have all that stuff?" She waved toward the doorway. "We walked through five rooms of stuff piled floor-to-ceiling. Why do you hoard it?"

"I don't hoard it. I collect it. What would you have me do with it? Give it away?"

"Sure, or sell it."

"It's mine," he said simply. "I won it and if I want to pile it up, then I can pile it up. It has no meaning other than that."

"So you brought Applegate here to store with the rest of your forgotten prizes?" She put her elbows on the table and contemplated him.

"I'm a gambler," he said and forked up a bite of roast. "I win things. What I do with my winnings is no one's business but my own."

"It must have taken a long time to accumulate all this."

"I learned how to play cards at a very early age. It was just a matter of time before I won this estate and everything in it."

She tried not to think of herself as part of his winnings. It was hard enough knowing that Applegate was. Her horse deserved better.

"When did you win this place?"

"Before the war," he said.

"Have you done anything with the grounds?"

"To what purpose?" he asked and finished his roast. "I'm not the kind of man to work with his hands."

"You don't have to be," she said with a shake of her head. "You have so many things, you could sell some of it and hire people to take care of the place."

"The Strasburgs do a fine job. The house isn't falling down. The fences get repaired. The animals are well cared for. What else is there?"

"You could breed horses," she said with exasperation. "Or you could have a whole herd of fine dairy cattle and sell milk and cheeses at market. I bet there are crofters' houses on this estate, aren't there?"

"A few."

"See? With some vision and a little work, you could have ensured a future for your children."

He leaned in closer to her with an odd look on his face. "I never planned to have children so there was no need to worry about their future."

"But all that has changed now."

"How so?"

"We're married," she said. "We'll have children."

He raised a dark eyebrow in her direction. "One does not necessarily lead to the other."

"Of course it does," she said. "That's why one gets married, to have children and build a family."

"That is certainly *not* why we got married."

She had the good grace to blush. "You could have said no."

"Right, I could have refused you at the altar and then you and *my* horse would have gone back home no worse for wear." He crossed his arms over his chest. "I'm not in the habit of giving my things away."

"So you married me and brought me here to add to your collection?" She waved her hand to emphasize her point.

"No, I married you and brought Applegate here to add to my collection."

"I won't stay in this house like a bearskin rug or a . . . a . . . moose head."

"Fine, suit yourself. I'm sure your family will be happy to take you back." He leaned back and insolently blinked at her. "You're no worse for wear."

"I—I will not leave Applegate. I am not in the habit of leaving someone I love."

"Applegate is a horse, not a someone." His tone was suddenly sober and sincere.

"I was there when Applegate was born," she said, and stood. "To me, he is more than just a horse. That's why I couldn't let you take him away. I know you can't fathom that kind of devotion, so I'm not asking you to. As I've stated before, I would be quite content to sleep outside in the barn with my horse. As long as he is cared for, I won't bother you. Truly, you won't even know I exist."

"Oh, I'll know you exist," he said and stood, towering over her. "So will the neighbors. I won't have them thinking I keep pretty young gals locked up in my barn."

"No, you'll simply keep me locked up in your house."

At that very moment the storm hit. Lightning flashed outside the door, spooking Amelia. The wind picked up—if that was possible—and howled down the wide chimney causing the banked fire to sputter and flare.

The door rattled furiously with the wind and Alex looked from it to her. Anger and some other emotion she could not decipher gleamed in his eyes. "The locks on my doors work from the inside. I suggest you use them."

He stormed across the room, his mood obviously as black as the weather outside. He grabbed his jacket and hat. "I'm not locking you in, but I won't be responsible for you if you go out in this storm."

"I thought you took care of what was yours." She spit the words back in his face.

"You are a little fool." He pulled on his jacket and opened the door.

The storm greeted him with a curtain of wild driving rain. He glanced her way one last time and shoved his hat down on his head. Then he disappeared into the storm.

What had he gotten himself into?

Alex shrugged off his coat and stretched out on the cot that was always ready in the tack room. It was there for the times when an animal was sick or a mare in foal and twenty-four-hour attention was needed. He and Mr. Strasburg would take turns resting.

Alex studied the shadows on the ceiling. There was a small four-paned window in the tack room. The glass was expensive, but it allowed in the light, and now the lightning made shadows jump around the room.

The slate ceiling was dry. The air was fragrant with the scent of hay, horses and well-used leather, and the blankets under him were rough, sturdy wool. Outside the storm screamed with laughter as if the elements were making fun of his dilemma.

He frowned. He hadn't planned on getting a wife. It had just happened. The stubborn gal was supposed to have called it off, and let him take his horse and go.

He turned and stared at the window. He was married now. That meant that he was responsible for another human being. Someone who would lie and cheat and eventually leave him. It was a lesson he had learned a long time ago. One he had vowed never to have to learn again. Yet here he was, married.

Strange as it seemed, it was his wedding night and he was stuck out in the barn because he had some sense of honor. He rolled over and punched the feather pillow in a futile attempt to make it more comfortable.

He thought about Amelia, her lovely body dressed only in a nightgown, resting between his sheets, in his bed. Her hair would be spread out like silk. Her sweet mouth slightly open. She smelled like candy. She would leave her candy scent on the sheets.

Shoot, it was suddenly very hot. Alex took off his shirt and tossed it onto a peg. Then he took off his boots and lay back down. Maybe she was hot too, he wondered. Maybe the bed covers would be too warm and she would toss them off. Or better yet, perhaps she would take off her night clothes and leave only the cool cotton sheets to caress her soft skin and firm curves.

The storm whipped up in response to his ridiculous thoughts. Alex stared at the ceiling. He had to think of something else or he would never get to sleep.

She was so innocent. She hadn't even thought about the fact that she was pledging herself to a stranger.

Someone should have taught her the ways of the world. The same way he had taught her brother about gambling. What if she had married herself off to a man with a black heart? What if he had been the kind to hurt her? What if he had been a drunk?

She had simply looked at him like he was crazy when he mentioned the possibilities. Of course, Alex wasn't a drunk and he would never force himself on a gal, but she didn't know that.

What he wanted was to get a hold of her father and tell him a thing or two about leaving his naive children alone in the world.

Alex tried to imagine her father. He couldn't really picture the man. Perhaps he had beaten her. Alex didn't like where his thoughts were taking him. Perhaps her home life had been so bad she was glad to latch onto the first guy who dressed well and looked clean.

Alex had left a note for Robert Morgan with the sheriff. When the man got back to town, Alex would be the first to know. Then he'd find out a thing or two. Either her father was an idiot who didn't know how to care for his children, or he was a beast.

If the man had any decency, he'd come running for Amelia with his guns blazing, demanding that the marriage be annulled. Alex knew what he would do when that happened. He would annul it of course. That had been his back-up plan from the start. He always had a backup plan.

He put his hands behind his head and let out a long low breath. Of course, he couldn't touch her if he planned to annul the marriage. So he had to stop thinking about her.

He turned his mind to what he would do if he discovered her father was a beast. He'd beat the tar out of him, of course, and then he would annul and send Amelia on her way with a bigger dowry. That way she could take her time and marry someone who loved her. He already knew she deserved that much.

Alex also knew he was a cynic, but that didn't mean he was heartless. From what her brother had said, Amelia's father would be home in a few short weeks. Then the issue would be settled. It wasn't so bad. He simply had to take care of Amelia until her father came. Then Alex would set her safely aside and return to the life he had planned. The life that left him responsible for no one but himself.

That was that. He would have this outrageous marriage annulled. All he had to do was stay away from her for a few weeks. How hard could that be?

Amelia tossed and turned on the big feather bed. She told herself it was the storm that kept her awake. But as if to prove otherwise, the wind grew stronger and popped open the window. She flung the smooth cotton sheets off, climbed out of bed and pushed it closed. The sash was wet from the driving rain and she stepped into an icy puddle on the floor beneath it.

She ignored her cold feet and stared out at the stable. The rain poured onto its slate roof. A thin wisp of smoke was quickly blown away from the small chimney by a gust of wind. She wondered how Applegate was doing in his new home.

She bit her bottom lip and admitted that she really wanted to know how Alex was doing too. Honestly, she admitted, it was guilt that kept her awake more than the storm. She had practically forced the man to marry her and now he felt compelled to sleep in the stable.

Why? Because he was a good man. He had seen the look of determination on her face when she declared she would live in the barn. By sleeping in the stable, he kept her from being ridiculed by the neighbors.

Amelia sighed long and loud. He had called her a little fool and he was right. After all, she only married the man to be close to Applegate. She turned her back on the storm and stared at the darkened room. It was huge by comparison to any room she had ever slept in and, like all the other rooms she had peered into, it was filled from floor to ceiling.

How could he think he might lose all this? It seemed clear he stockpiled things just to say he had them. But he should enjoy them. *He* should be sleeping in this big feather bed. Not her.

She had been too stubborn to let her brother face his own consequences and as a result, had ruined Alex's life. She had stolen his chance to fall in love and marry the woman of his dreams. She had robbed him of the kind of love she read about in books. The kind of love she had seen her sister Madeline find.

Amelia hadn't thought about any of this when she forced Alex's hand. All she'd thought about was the fact that he was going to take Applegate away. That she would no longer have a dowry and a reason for someone to fall in love with her. Her motives in this fiasco had been purely selfish.

Guilt weighed heavily on her heart. She wondered if she could make it up to Alex somehow. But how do you repay a man for such a loss? She stared at the storm outside the window.

The answer came to her in the next flash of lightning. She squared her shoulders and tried to be brave. The answer was quite clear. She would have to be the best wife a man could ever want. Perhaps if she tried hard enough, he would fall in love with her and if he fell in love, his life would no longer be ruined. She would be redeemed.

Amelia liked the idea. She paced in front of the window. How exactly could she get a man to fall in love with her? All she knew about love was what she had learned from watching her sisters.

Men fell in love with her baby sister Beth all the time. All

Beth had to do was walk into a room and men fell to their knees, their hearts quickly at her feet.

Amelia made a face. No man had ever had that reaction to her. Besides, Alex had already seen her so it wasn't going to be love at first sight. She clenched her hands behind her back and pondered as she paced. What did Beth do to get that reaction?

Amelia thought for a while and realized that Beth always did her hair and wore only her best gowns. She made a point to always look her best whenever a man was around. Amelia had thought it silly, but Beth said it was important to look one's best at all times. What else did she go on about? Oh yes, according to Beth men liked women to smell exotic.

Well, Amelia could do that. She just never took the time before. She glanced at the wardrobe she had emptied and hung her things inside. Henry had packed three of her best dresses along with her toilet items and her peppermint hand cream. It wasn't as if she had nothing to wear but her riding outfit. She could make an effort to look her best but even then she would never be the beauty Beth was. She tapped her chin. What if Alex had dreamed of marrying a beauty?

Amelia was honest with herself. No amount of pretty ribbon or honeyed face cream would make her a beauty. Shoot, this was going to be hard.

What else did she know of love? Trevor had fallen in love with Maddie. How did that work? Maddie was almost twenty-five, so it wasn't her youth and beauty that had done it. What exactly had Maddie done?

Amelia turned and paced some more. Maddie had lived with Trevor's family. Of course, he thought she was going to marry his brother, but there must be something about being in close quarters that makes a man fall in love. It probably didn't hurt that Maddie is the best cook in the county.

Amelia could cook, in fact she considered herself to be quite good. She had never entered the County Fair cook-offs because she hadn't wanted to compete against Maddie.

She looked out the window at the stable so far away and frowned. Proximity was a problem. Alex would never fall in love with her if he stayed in the stable. Somehow she had to get and keep him closer to her. How was she supposed to do that?

There was so much to think about, so much to consider. The only way she knew to deal with a problem was to form a plan, and the only way to form a plan was to write down her thoughts and organize them. What she needed to do was make a list.

Amelia went to the nightstand, got out her glasses, propped them on her nose, and lit the lamp she had brought upstairs with her. There was a writing desk next to the window, oddly enough with only a few boxes on it. She took them down and rummaged through the nooks and crannies of the desk. She ran her hand over the inlaid mahogany checkered with lines scrolling around the writing area.

She opened the top of the desk to find parchment and an ink well inside. The well was firmly capped and the ink fresh enough to use. She pulled out the chair and sat down. Taking out a piece of parchment, she dipped the fine-pointed pen in the ink well and titled her thoughts, "How to Make a Man Fall in Love With You."

Then she wrote the number one. Tapping the pen against her chin she thought about her sister Beth and wrote: "Always take the time to look your best. 2. Smell pretty." Then she thought about her sister Madeline. "3. Impress him with your cooking" and "4. Proximity is key."

She stared at the paper. If these were truly the ways to a man's heart, then she wasn't doing very well. After an afternoon of riding, her hair had been tumbling about, her boots still smelled of the barn, and worse, her clothes smelled of horse. No wonder it hadn't been love at first sight.

She sighed. She wasn't doing so well with the other numbers, either. Not only had she looked a mess, but now her victim, er, husband, was one hundred yards away, sleeping in the stable. She shook her head. There had to be more she could do.

She thought of her brother Robert. He said that he was in love with a gal down in Wellsville. What was it about her that he liked? Oh yes, she always agreed with him.

Amelia sighed again. If she had agreed with Alex, then she wouldn't be in this mess. He would have Applegate and that would be that. She shook her head and wrote, "5. Agree with him whenever possible." Okay. That was something she could work on.

Her brother Griffin liked a girl who enjoyed the same things he did. That wasn't bad. Alex was a gambler and she was pretty handy at cards. "6. Share common interests."

She stared at the paper. There had to be something else. Something she was missing. She struggled, her thoughts tumbling through all the stories she had read. Sleeping Beauty fit under number one. The prince had fallen in love with her at first sight. Cinderella also fit under this one. She sighed. What Amelia wouldn't do for a fairy godmother right about now.

There was a sound out in the corridor and Amelia jumped. Had she wished a fairy godmother into existence? Or had Alex decided that a feather bed would be more comfortable than a cot in the stable?

She had no idea what to do if he did. Picking up the lamp, she crossed the room. "Hello? Who's out there?"

There was no answer.

She opened her door and looked out into the crowded hall. "Hello? Is anyone there?"

Two long minutes and no answer. The storm must have caused the sound, she reasoned. It might have blown open another window in the house. Alex's warning ran through her mind. *"The locks work from the inside. I suggest you use them."* She swallowed her doubts, gave the shadows in the hall one last look, then closed the door and turned the key in the lock.

Somewhat unnerved, she went back to her desk and studied her list. It wasn't very convincing. There had to be more to it than that. For the first time in her life, she wished she had paid more attention to Beth's rambling twitters about boys.

She sighed and put away her writing. Another glance out the window told her that the storm was finally weakening. The windup clock on the desk showed that it was after 2:00 A.M. Too late to do anything about Alex now. Her plan would have to wait.

She climbed back into the big bed, put her glasses on the nightstand and turned down the lamp. In the morning the skies would be clear and everything would be fresh. She would see to it that she dressed in her best morning outfit. Then she would fix Alex a nice breakfast. A meal that would prove what a good cook she was. She turned onto her side and curled up. Hadn't she heard somewhere that the way to a man's heart was through his stomach?

If that was the case, perhaps she had a chance at redemption after all. She smiled and closed her eyes. In the morning her quest would begin. With any luck, by this time next week Alex Laird would have fallen in love with her and she would be redeemed.

Alex was up at dawn. His eyes were sunken from the lack of sleep. He pumped fresh icy water into a basin and dunked his head in it. The water shocked him, instantly waking him up and numbing his skin. He growled at the pain and shook his head, then reached for a towel.

With the thick cotton cloth, he dried his face and slicked back his hair. He opened his eyes to a vision in pink standing next to him. He blinked in an attempt to clear the vision, but she was still there.

"Good morning," Amelia said cheerfully. He took a step back and bumped against the cot. It knocked him off balance enough to make him have to sit down. The cot caught his weight with a gentle "woof."

"Oh, I didn't mean to startle you," she said, a look of concern flashing across her beautiful face.

"What are you doing here?" he managed to ask. "Why are you dressed like that?" He waved toward Amelia's gown. It was pale pink with a full hoop skirt that took up most of the floor in the small tack room. She looked as if she were a fine lady ready to go on a picnic. He'd seen such a spectacle down South but never around here and never anywhere near a stable.

"I came to invite you to breakfast," she said. "What would you like?"

"I don't eat breakfast," he replied and studied the frock. It was a ridiculously fancy thing, made more so by the tack room setting. Her dark auburn hair was done up in elaborate twists, exposing the stubborn line of her jaw above her long, pale neck.

A pulse beat there, just under the soft skin where her neck met the collarbone. It was a sweet sexy pulse that made a man think things he shouldn't be thinking this early in the morning.

"Don't be silly," she said and took a step toward him. He leaned back against the wall trying to keep some distance from the temptress in front of him. "Everyone eats breakfast. Now what would you like? Ham, bacon, sausages? I could make eggs. I also make a mean biscuit if you'd like biscuits and gravy."

"Mrs. Strasburg cooks," he said. "It's her job, not yours and she knows I don't eat breakfast."

"Oh." A look of disappointment flashed through Amelia's beautiful eyes. "How about lunch? I know this great recipe for leg of lamb."

Alex stood up. He was well aware of the fact that he was wearing only his pants. His shirt, vest and jacket hung over the chair behind her. His boots sat beside the door frame.

Standing up brought him dangerously close to Amelia. The soft fabric of her skirt brushed his knees. The scent of peppermint candy filled the air. He was a full head taller and the vantage point brought the pale skin of her collar bone closer. The bodice of her dress dipped tantalizingly low, showing enough curve to make his mouth go dry.

"Alex?"

"What?"

"Lunch?"

"What?"

"Do you want leg of lamb for lunch?"

What he wanted to do was kiss that spot where her neck met her shoulder and see if her skin tasted like candy. He blinked. He had to get out of there or his plan for annulment would be forgotten. "I won't be home for lunch," he said and pushed his way around her skirts to get his clothes.

Frustration washed over her face. She stuck her hands on her hips emphasizing her tiny waist and he had to turn his back on her. She was visibly trembling with emotion just like she had the day before. It caused his sleep-deprived brain to contemplate all kinds of things he had no business thinking about.

"Will you be home for dinner?"

He knew she was put out from the tone of her voice. Ignoring it, he stuffed his arms in his shirt and pulled it over his head. "Don't wait dinner for me," he said evenly. "Mrs. Strasburg always leaves something on the stove."

Once he had tucked in his shirt and slipped on his vest he turned back to the seductress behind him. She did not look happy and it tugged at his heart. He reached for his jacket. The motion brought him within close range of her smooth skin. She practically stood in his arms. He couldn't help himself. He dropped a small kiss on her shoulder near the spot he really wanted to taste.

It was a big mistake. She tasted much better than candy. He clenched his hands for a moment, grabbed his jacket, scooped up his boots, and stepped out of the room.

"Just because we're married, doesn't mean you have to feed me," he said. "You'll be more successful looking after Applegate."

A safer distance away, he stopped and jammed his feet into his boots trying not to think about the taste of her. "And don't think just because I'm not around that you can take off with Applegate, either." He gave her a stern look and pulled on his jacket. "The stallion is mine. If you leave my property with him, I'll have the sheriff after you. They hang horse thieves around here—*men and women*."

She stood in the doorway, her mouth opening and closing as if she wanted to say something but couldn't find the proper words. Maybe it was the kiss that knocked her off her game.

He gave a mental shrug. If one kiss could distract her, then maybe a second one wouldn't hurt. That said, he stepped forward, crowding her against the tack room door frame. "Have fun today," he whispered and planted a kiss on the sweet spot just under her ear. "Don't do anything I wouldn't do."

She stared at him, dazed, and he turned and walked away, his heart light and his mood uplifted. The answer to his problem was clear. All he had to do to keep from being tempted was to kiss her speechless and make a quick getaway.

Yep, he was pretty certain he could do that until her father showed up. It solved his problem in a nice, neat fashion and neither one of them would be the worse for wear.

## Chapter Five

He had kissed her.

She had gotten up before dawn and put on her best dress. She had fixed her hair and pinched color into her cheeks. She had even offered to cook him the breakfast of his choice. For her efforts, he kissed her not once but twice. For a brief moment her hopes had risen, only to be dashed when he left her.

Kisses or not, Alex Laird had walked out of the stable as if he couldn't wait to be away from her. She was left hanging. Had her plan worked or not? She glanced at her dress. It was pressed. She sniffed her shoulder. She smelled like peppermint, which had to be considered more palatable than the stable. What had gone wrong?

She sat down on a bale of hay. Since she was alone it didn't matter that she flopped down, unmindful of the skirts that billowed around her. Frowning she put her elbows on her knees and dropped her chin onto her palms and fought confusion and despair. So much for her grand plan. It was obvious that step one, *always look your best*, hadn't made one whit of difference.

Step three, *stay in close proximity*, was impossible if the man kept running off. And just exactly how was she supposed to win his heart through his stomach if he didn't eat?

Redemption was going to be harder than she had thought. She didn't know what she had expected when she entered the tack room, but the idea Alex Laird might be half naked and dripping wet had never crossed her mind. She blinked. It certainly was burned into her mind now.

The room had been so small that even without her glasses she had gotten a good look at him. She closed her eyes and conjured up the sight. Alex was tall and his muscular shoulders were broad and well-defined. She wanted to run her fingers along their contours. That was a problem with her, she liked to touch things. It helped to cement her memories.

Then when he'd dried off with the towel and slicked his thick dark hair away from his face, she had wanted to drool. Which is definitely not lady-like. Honestly, she had never seen anything so handsome in all her life.

Just before he'd opened his eyes, she had watched a droplet of water run off his hair, over his solid jaw, and along the column of his neck where it merrily skimmed across his shoulder and down his contoured chest. Right then she had wished to be that droplet. The thought made her knees go weak.

Then he'd opened his eyes and looked at her. She must have been staring like a ninny because she'd had to try hard to remember she had a mission. So she had blurted out her announcement about breakfast.

Of course, he wasn't buying her ruse. A look of suspicion had crossed his face just before he'd informed her that he didn't eat breakfast.

She hadn't known what to do after that. Breakfast was an important part of her plan—a plan that was shot down before she had even gotten started. So she had leaped on the idea of a big lunch, which hadn't worked either.

She had not known what else to say. The tack room was quite small and the setting intimate. She had never seen a man dress before. It was a scene she wouldn't soon forget.

Nor would she forget the kiss he'd so casually planted on her collarbone or the heart-stopping moment when he'd come back to her and made gooseflesh rise along her neck. That last touch of his lips still had her tingling. It was clear that Alex knew his way around women. He simply wasn't interested in falling in love with *her*.

She leaned back against the wall and closed her eyes. Somehow she had to get his interest. The dress hadn't worked. Neither had the offer of a meal. She was stumped.

Too bad there wasn't a manual about this, a book of love that would give her some clue as to what to do. She opened her eyes. It wasn't a bad idea. Perhaps there was a library in town. Perhaps, just perhaps the librarian knew of a book that might help her.

She stood up and brushed the hay off her gown. Ever optimistic, she knew what she had to do. She would change into her riding habit and take Applegate to the nearest town. An afternoon at the library would be just the thing to help her out.

She stopped at the door. Alex had warned her not to ride off the property. Well, that certainly put a kink in her plans. She stomped her foot in frustration and glanced over her shoulder at the long row of stalls. Alex had specified that she couldn't ride Applegate off the property, but that didn't mean she couldn't take *another* horse. She smiled at her own cleverness. Amelia was familiar with demanding men. Her household was full of them. Dealing with Alex would be no different. She'd prove that today when she went into town.

\* \* \*

Alex folded his hand of cards and stood up. "Sorry, gentlemen."

"What's with him?" Charlie Johnson asked while keeping a thick cigar firmly clenched between his teeth.

"Maybe his luck had turned," Bryant Haggle replied with a smirk.

Alex wasn't sure what was wrong with him. He felt distracted. It was as if he could feel his luck turning sour. On days like that it was best if he walked away from the game. Maybe a change of scenery was needed.

He could go up to Milwaukee and try his hand at a game or two up there. He was a member of a club for wealthy gentlemen up there. It was where he usually happened upon his best hands.

He rubbed his hand across his face and stepped out of the saloon. First, what he really needed was a good cup of black coffee. Millie Winkle ran a diner a few doors down. She was always good for a nice flirt and a thick cup of hot brew.

A flirt. His thoughts went straight to a lady in pink and the sweet candy taste of her warm skin. What was really bothering him was the idea that all that sweetness was his for the taking.

He shook his head. He wasn't going to be suckered in. If he tasted her, he would be stuck with her forever. It wouldn't be fair to her and it wouldn't be fair to him.

He only had to make it the few weeks until her father came to get her. He vowed to give her an annulment and a fair chance at a real life. Alex knew being married to a gambler was no life for a lady. Amelia was simply too naive to realize that.

He was headed down the street toward the diner when he caught a familiar movement out of the corner of his eye. He turned and slipped into the shadows of a nearby alley to get a better look. It was Amelia. She had changed into the riding outfit from the day before.

Alex frowned. Was she leaving? Didn't she believe him when he said he'd have her hanged as a horse thief?

He leaned against the building and watched her. She dismounted and led one of his mares through the town, taking in the store fronts and buildings. It was clear she was looking for something . . . or someone.

Alex straightened himself and stepped into the street. If he had to he would drag her all the way back home. She walked right past him as if she didn't see him standing there in the semi-crowded street.

It bothered him to no end that he had picked her out just by the way she moved, yet she looked right through him as she passed by.

He pushed his way through two people and around a wagon hauling barrels until he matched her step by step. "What are you doing?"

She jumped nearly a foot and put her hand on her breast as she blinked at him through her glasses. Glasses she had not worn that morning. "Oh, my goodness, Alex, you startled me." She frowned at him. "You have to stop sneaking up on me."

"I didn't sneak up," he said. "I walked with you nearly half a block before I said anything. Now, why don't you tell me what you think you're doing?"

"I'm looking for a library," she said. "Does this town have one?"

"What do you need a library for?"

She turned the most interesting shade of pink. "Well, I was looking for a book."

"What kind of book?"

"Um . . . a . . ." She touched the tip of her tongue to her

bottom lip. The motion stopped Alex in his tracks. He had to remind himself to breathe. "I'm looking for a . . . reference book."

He shook himself and tried to get a grip on his rampant emotions. "There's a whole library full of books at the house. You're more likely to find the book you're looking for there than in a small-town library."

"You have a library?"

"Sure, didn't you bother to look around?"

"Well, um, you see . . . I went out for a bit of morning exercise, saw the town . . . and I thought I'd check out the library."

"I thought I told you not to ride off the property."

"You told me not to ride Applegate off the property," she countered, her gaze never leaving the road. "So I borrowed this lovely mare instead."

"Hello, Angel." Alex reached up and patted the mare on the nose. The animal nodded and nudged him until he pulled a sugar cube out of his pocket and gave the old girl a treat. "I'd prefer you didn't ride off the property without me."

"Why ever not?"

"It's not safe," he said simply.

"I can take care of myself."

"How can you say that? You don't know these people or this area. This animal is clearly worth a man's life. There are many unscrupulous people who wouldn't even think twice about taking yours."

"Why do you think so poorly of people?"

"Why do you think so highly?" he countered.

"People have always been kind to me."

"Then you've been living in an ivory tower. I want you to go back home."

"Why?"

"Why? Because I say so."

She glanced around and Alex saw that they were drawing

curious stares. "Are you afraid of being seen with me?" she whispered. "Because if you are, than you should have thought about that before you married me."

He leaned toward her and lowered his voice. "What I want is for my wife to take my horse and go home. As my wife, you must do as I say."

"I have to tell you that I do not plan on spending the rest of my life being ordered around by you. I have had enough of that from my father."

"You should have thought about that before you married me."

She glared at him. "I do not understand you."

He straightened and crossed his arms over his chest. "I don't care if you understand me or not. What I care about is that you listen to me."

"Hey, Laird," Charlie shouted from the saloon door. "You got a problem?"

"No problem," Alex tossed over his shoulder. He turned and looked at Amelia. "Just a wife." He said it so that she was the only one who could hear it.

"Nice horse," Charlie went on hollering. "Is it new?"

"I acquired her last month."

"Must have been a real lucky hand."

"Not lucky enough," Alex muttered under his breath. He decided that he didn't like all the attention they were getting, so he took Amelia by the arm and led both her and the mare back toward the saloon to retrieve his mount. "Come on, I'm taking you home."

"You don't have to bother," she said through clenched teeth. "I know the way."

"I suppose you do know the way." He stopped her next to his horse. "But I don't trust you to do what I asked."

"You didn't ask," she said and crossed her arms under her breasts emphasizing her curves. "You demanded."

"Honey, it's a man's right to demand things of his wife." Alex picked her up by the waist and tossed her onto her saddle. She was light and warm and for the briefest of moments, far too close to him. "You're lucky I'm not very demanding," he finished.

He took hold of Angel's reins and mounted his own horse. His gelding snorted, but Alex was not in the mood for animal shenanigans. He took both horses firmly in hand and headed out of town.

Amelia thought she would die of embarrassment. Alex had tossed her up on the horse as if she were a petulant ten-year-old. She might be innocent but she was pretty certain there was another meaning to his words. *Demand things of his wife.*

Was he mad because he had slept out in the stable? He was the one who made a big production out of it. It wasn't her fault he didn't sleep in his bed. When she'd offered to cook for him, he wasn't interested. So what else did he mean by making demands of his wife?

He didn't speak again until they were in front of his stable. An elderly man stepped out the door as Alex dismounted.

"Mr. Laird, I didn't expect to see you here this early."

"Wasn't having much luck in town," Alex said. "How's my new stallion doing?"

"He's a feisty one," the white-haired old man said, "but a beauty."

"He's the finest stallion my father has produced so far. His daddy was a racer and his mama was known for her calmness." Alex helped Amelia dismount. As soon as her feet touched the ground, she took a step away from him. Right now she was not happy with the man. It seemed the only thing she could do to please him was to meekly be at his beck and call. The idea did not to appeal to her. In fact, she doubted she could dredge up enough guilt over this marriage to even begin to feel meek.

"Bert, this is my wife, Amelia," Alex said off-handedly. "Amelia, this is Bert Strasburg. If you need anything when I'm gone, you go to Bert before you go running into town."

"I'm sure Mr. Strasburg has better things to do than to run errands for me," Amelia said and shook the old man's hand. "Applegate loves carrots right before bedtime."

"I'll remember that," the old man said and took the horses' reins. "He has the look of good stock. Are you going to breed him, Mr. Laird?"

"I haven't decided yet."

"Of course he's going to breed him," Amelia said. "Applegate was born to found a dynasty."

"A dynasty?" Alex asked. "That might be, but I haven't decided if I'm going to keep him."

"Of course you'll keep him!" Amelia said. "How could you not?"

"Like I said, Bert, I don't know what I'm going to do with him."

Astounded, Amelia stomped her foot. "You will keep him. I won't hear of you selling him."

"He's mine to keep or sell," Alex said and bent down so that he was nose to nose with her. "Get that idea through your thick little head right now. Applegate is mine. I can breed him, sell him or destroy him if I've a mind to."

"You would never!" Amelia could not believe Alex would be so cruel. "You'll have to kill me first."

"It can be arranged."

Amelia gasped in outrage and watched as Alex marched off toward the house.

"He won't kill him," the old man said.

Amelia turned to the stable manager. The man was not

much taller than Amelia. Thick-waisted and dressed in heavy wool pants and a flannel shirt, he looked more like an elf than a stable manager. His round face and snow-white beard accented blue eyes that danced with speculation.

"He might sell him, though. Mr. Laird ain't known for keeping things."

"Have you seen the inside of his house lately?" she asked her arms akimbo. The old man's eyes twinkled. "Have you?"

"Of course I have," he said.

"That tells me the only reason Alex would sell my stallion is to get back at me." The old man didn't disagree and Amelia sighed. "Well, I refuse to let him sell Applegate. A man has to listen to his wife, doesn't he?"

"Now if you had asked me that in front of the missus, I'd a had to say yes. But, seeing as she ain't around here, I'm going to give it to you straight. A man will do what a man wants to do regardless of what anyone else thinks . . . even his wife."

"Well!" Amelia said affronted by the man's opinion.

He smiled at her. "Congratulations, by the way."

"For what?"

"For marryin' the biggest confirmed bachelor in the whole state of Wisconsin. If you don't mind my asking, how'd you do it?"

"It's a long story."

The old man chuckled and pulled the horses toward the stable. "Now that's a story I might want to hear sometime."

"I'm sure it's not as interesting as you think."

"Oh, somehow I believe it is." He disappeared into the stable. Amelia felt a cold breeze brush down her neck. She shivered and headed toward the house.

Alex said he had a room full of books. Probably more books than any library near here. She bit her bottom lip and went inside. Hopefully he had a book in there somewhere that would tell her what she needed to do.

Right now she didn't much care that she was failing at the whole falling-in-love thing. Which was bad. "Bad, bad, bad," she muttered as she walked up the slope to the kitchen door.

Amelia needed to care, because if a man was truly in love there wasn't anything he wouldn't do for his woman, including keeping Applegate and founding a dynasty. Therefore, she reasoned, love might be the only chance she had to keep her dreams alive.

That little gal was going to drive him to drink. Alex pushed through a few stacks of boxes that stood between him and the small bar in his den. To heck with her driving him, it was after lunch and he was going to have a drink. He reached over a big box, grabbed a glass and a decanter full of his best Irish whiskey.

"Alex, are you in there? We need to talk."

He glanced up to see the top of her head peeking out between the boxes. She moved toward him at a pace that told him she was not happy. Well, neither was he. He did the very thing any other man would do in this situation. He climbed up the mountain of boxes and poured himself a shot.

"Alex! You're drinking!" she admonished as she stopped below him, hands on her hips.

"So?"

"So, you can't drink that."

"Watch me," he said and put the glass to his lips.

She gasped. "Stop it. It's too early. What will the Strasburgs think?"

"They'll think I must have been drinking when I married

you." He waved the glass around in front of him to emphasize his point.

"I won't have them thinking I married a drunk."

"Trust me, I'm not drunk . . . yet."

"Alex Laird, if you so much as sip that drink I'm going to—"

"What?" he asked and lifted the glass to his lips. "Leave me?"

"And let you have Applegate? I don't think so." She climbed the nearest box. "I will however come up there and take that drink away."

"Try." He grinned and stood up, lifting the glass high over his head.

Angry, she scrambled up the boxes. That alone was a sight to see. In her pique, her auburn hair slipped out of its pins. She had to raise her skirts high to step up from box to box. It gave him an interesting view of her firm calves clad in dark silk.

He hadn't seen legs that good since he'd dated that dance hall girl in San Francisco. The memory made his pulse race. He watched with fascination as she figured out the best path to get to him. She gave him a determined look that shot clear through to his soul.

He grinned and moved to the highest point on the mountain of boxes. Taking the stopper off the decanter, he splashed more whiskey into the glass. The movement infuriated her. Her eyes turned stormy behind her glasses and she trembled in that most interesting way. Too bad all that passion was anger. There was a thing or two he could teach her about passion that was much more fun.

"I cannot believe you are being so stubborn," she said. "I swear you are no better than my brothers."

"No, Honey, I am better. I'm the one with the horse, remember?"

"How could I forget." She eyed the boxes still between them. "This is ridiculous."

"I agree. A man should be able to have a drink in his own house without being chastised."

For a sweet moment she looked guilty. Then her gaze settled on the nearly overflowing glass in his hand. "You aren't drinking. You're deliberately baiting me. You've been baiting me since we met."

"And you've responded so well," he said and took a serious swallow out of the glass. The heat from the whiskey settled into his stomach, easing the tension in his shoulders. He could finish the drink, but he was having second thoughts. It wouldn't do for him to fall off this stupid mountain of boxes. Or worse, lose his inhibitions, climb down and make love to his pretty new bride. Lord, if he did that all heck would break loose.

Just to spite her, he poured more whiskey into the shot glass.

She was beside him when he looked up. Heat radiated off of her. Her breathing was erratic and did nice things to her chest. Before he could comment, she snatched the glass out of his hand. "Hey!"

She held the glass out over the edge of the boxes. "I asked you not to drink."

He shrugged and pulled the decanter toward his lips. She gasped when he lifted it to drink. Her anger radiated off of her in waves. All that emotion sure made her compelling.

"If you drink that, then I'll drink this," she warned. "I swear I will."

He arched an eyebrow at her challenge. "Go ahead."

"What?!"

"I said go ahead. You look like you could use a drink."

"You're bluffing."

"Am I?"

"You wouldn't want your wife to be drinking in the middle of the afternoon, would you?"

"As long as you don't fall ill . . ."

"You are horrid."

"I never promised that I'd be a gentleman." He patted the box next to him. "Come on, sit. If you plan on drinking with me, then you'd better be sitting down. We're rather high to risk falling."

He watched as she calculated how close she would have to be to him to actually sit. She looked over the edge of the boxes. The ceilings in the house were ten feet tall. Sitting, his head was mere inches from the ceiling. The way he figured it a fall from that height might break something. Unless, of course, one was drunk.

He lifted the decanter to his lips. The movement had its intended effect. She gasped, glared and tossed the whiskey back like an old pro. He waited a heartbeat. She blinked, tears welled up in her eyes and she sucked in a deep breath.

Her reaction was amusing until she started to lose her balance. He'd only been kidding about falling.

Alex grabbed her by the waist and mindful of the mere inches above his head, pulled her back into his lap. The motion rocked the top of the mound of boxes. He held on tight and prayed they wouldn't go down in a pile of dust.

"Oh, my," she said. Her arms were around his neck. Her face pressed into his shoulder. She smelled of whiskey and candy. Not an altogether bad combination. She felt good in his lap. Her riding costume was made of thick wool, but her stumble had drawn her skirts up around her knees, revealing cotton and silk undergarments.

He rested one hand on her corseted waist, the other on her leg just above the knee. She was soft to the touch. Her breasts were pressed against his chest. All in all, she fit him as well as any woman could.

He exhaled and resisted the urge to run his hand up and down her thigh. It was a very strong urge. He told himself it would be just to see how she would react, but then he couldn't do it.

She was shaking. The near fall had scared her half to death. The pulse at the base of her neck beat erratically.

"Are you all right?" he asked softly and buried his nose in her silky hair. She smelled so good.

"I think so," she said, but didn't let go of him.

He settled her more comfortably against him. "Never have a drink before?"

"Champagne," she said. Her breath was moist and unexpected against the side of his neck. It did strange things to his stomach.

"Whiskey's a bit different than champagne."

"More shocking than anything."

"Yeah, kind of takes your breath away the first time."

"The first time?"

"Sure, the second time, it's not so bad."

"I don't believe you." She sat up, pulling away from him. He didn't want her to go. The only way to get her to stay in his arms was to distract her.

"It's true," he said as solemnly as possible. "Here, have another swallow." He lifted the decanter to her lips.

"I couldn't possibly. It's the middle of the afternoon."

"Suit yourself," he said and with a shrug brought the whiskey to his lips. With a great show, he pretended to drink.

She tugged the bottle down. "You shouldn't be drinking either. Really, Alex, we need to talk."

"Okay, but only after you take another drink."

"I'm not a drinker."

"Neither am I. That's not the point."

"Then what is the point?"

"The point is that I am right but you won't believe me

unless you have proof." He lifted the decanter. "Take another sip and you will see that I am right. About the burning . . ."

She eyed him suspiciously. "What if I take a sip and disagree with you?"

"Then you disagree."

"And we'll talk."

"Fine, we'll talk."

She took the decanter in hand and tilted it up to her mouth. "Just a sip."

"Just a sip," he agreed. Something like satisfaction ran through him when she closed her eyes and did what he asked. It showed that she was beginning to trust him. Maybe being married wasn't as bad as he once thought.

## Chapter Six

She pretended to take a sip of the whiskey, just to prove to him that he was wrong. "It's still bad," she declared and handed him the decanter. "I hope you don't make a habit out of drinking."

She wiped her mouth with the back of her hand. Her lips burned and she felt the drink warming her stomach. "All this heat can't be good for a person."

"I rather like the heat," he said.

She blinked and realized where she sat. "Oh my, I'm sorry. I'm on your lap." Blushing, she scrambled off him.

"Watch it!" He grabbed her hand and pulled her down beside him.

"What?"

"You nearly bumped your head."

Amelia looked up. The ceiling was inches away. He had saved her yet again.

"I'm not usually so clumsy," she said. "It's just that when I'm around you I'm not myself."

"Why's that?"

"I wish I knew." She carefully folded her hands in her lap

79

and stared out across the room. Alex was so close it made her pulse race. It was oddly intimate at the top of the boxes as if they were above the whole world. She glanced at him. "You're not going to keep drinking are you?"

"No," he said and put the stopper on the decanter. "I'm not inclined to fall that far."

She smiled at him. "Me neither. Thank you for saving me."

"You're welcome."

He smelled like after shave and manliness with just a hint of horse. It was a comfortable scent, reminding her of her father and her brothers and yet it was different on Alex. Somehow it was much more attractive.

She realized that she was staring at him again and glanced away. "What room is this?"

"My den."

"How can you tell?" She eyed the stacks of boxes that looked just like the stacks in every room.

"It's as small as the ladies' parlor and there's a desk under here somewhere along with a fully-stocked bar." He lifted the glass container. "It's where I got this."

"Why don't you take care of all this?"

"What?"

"All this stuff. Don't you want to be able to sit down near the fire and enjoy a rest without these mountains of boxes?"

He shrugged. "Guess I don't really care to do it."

"Do you care if I do it?"

"Do what?"

"Clean out these rooms."

"I won't have you throwing away my things."

"I won't throw them away," she said. "I promise. In fact I'll catalogue them and make sure they are stored properly."

"Do you really want to do that?"

"I like to organize things," she said. She looked over the room and thought about her bedroom, the parlor, and the dining room. Her heartbeat quickened. It would be great fun to see what was under it all. She glanced at him.

He frowned as if uncertain.

"I swear I will not get rid of anything without your permission."

"Nothing? Not even a torn piece of paper?"

"Not even a torn piece of paper," she said. "I promise."

"Well, if you promise, then I suppose it's all right."

Excitement swept over her. "Wonderful. Now, there is a promise I would like from you."

He blew out his breath and muttered, "Here it comes."

"It's not bad, honestly," she said. "It's what I came in here to talk to you about. I would like your promise that I will get the first chance to buy Applegate . . . should you want to sell him." She rushed the last part and looked down to see that she was wringing her hands. She took a slow breath and relaxed.

"You can't buy him," he said his tone gentle. "We're married. If I sell him, then *we're* selling him."

She wanted to clunk him on the head. "Fine, then please let my father buy him first. Applegate means the world to me." She closed her mouth before she said too much. "Please."

He rubbed his hand across his face. "All right, if I decide to sell Applegate, I'll give your father the first chance."

Amelia's heart skipped. Joy filled her. She wanted to hug him and almost did. She was mere inches from doing so when she stopped. "Promise?"

"Fine, I promise."

"Thank you." She kept her reaction ladylike and simply squeezed his hand. "I promise you won't regret it."

"That's one heck of a promise."

She smiled at him. "You said there's a library somewhere in this house?"

"Yes. A library and a conservatory, a formal parlor, a family parlor, the ladies' parlor, this den, a smoking room, oh, and the grand ballroom of course."

"Of course," she said, breathless at the thought. "What do you do with all this space?"

"It's storage, of course," he said with a grin. "Come on, let's get down and I'll give you the grand tour."

He stood up, careful to remain bent over so that he wouldn't hit his head. When he made his way down a few boxes and could stand straight, he turned and took her hand.

His palm was warm and callused. Her gaze met his. It seemed her husband did more than just play cards all day. Radiating up her arm, the heat of his grip was firm yet gentle as he guided her down the boxes.

The trip down was more difficult than the trip up had been. Her head was lighter and her footing not so steady.

"Watch it now," he said when she wavered. He let go of her hand and held her by the waist to steady her.

Then he swung her off the boxes. For a brief and shining moment he held her against him. They were heart to heart, his mouth a mere fraction from hers. She glanced at his lips, remembering how they had felt against her skin.

A warmth that was not whiskey-induced spread through her. She rested her hands on his broad shoulders and could feel the sculpted muscles working. Time slowed. Her mouth went dry. She touched her tongue to her bottom lip to moisten it. The taste of whiskey on her tongue matched the scent of his breath.

Her heart pounded as he dipped his head and kissed her. He claimed her, at first teasingly then with deepening passion as he pulled her closer against him.

She marveled at her own reaction to his passion. She wound her hands around his neck, pulling him in as he held her close. Unknown emotions swirled in her head, and pierced her heart. The kiss felt so right.

Right was the only word she could wrap her brain around as he slowly and patiently tutored her in the ways of kissing. Tiny shocks racked her when he touched his tongue to the spot she had moistened. She gasped at the new sensation and he encouraged her to kiss him back.

Safe and secure in his arms, she followed his lead. It was like dancing. The kiss was boundless, absorbing her heart and soul. For a brief time she forgot everything but this man and the wonderful way he made her feel.

"Excuse me."

Through the fog of her thoughts, Amelia heard someone cough and apologize. Alex broke the kiss, gently setting her on her feet. The ground spun around her, but his hand on her waist ensured that she would not fall. It was a silent promise that he would keep her safe.

"Mrs. Strasburg," Alex said and cleared his throat. "I would like you to meet my wife. Amelia, this is Ernestine Strasburg."

Amelia focused on the tiny woman in front of her. If she thought Mr. Strasburg was an elf, then Mrs. Strasburg surely was one. The woman was short, perhaps five feet tall with heels. She was as round-faced as her husband. Her skin was porcelain with a lovely pink blush in her cheeks.

She wore a housecap over her hair, but a long gray curl escaped to frame her face. Cheerful blue eyes twinkled as she smiled. "Well, a pleasure to meet you, Mrs. Laird."

"Amelia," she said and took the older woman's hand. "Please call me Amelia."

"Amelia, then." She clasped her hands in front of her and looked the two of them over. There was such an expression of glee on her face that it made Amelia wonder. "When was the happy event?" She pinned Alex with a not-so-happy look. "Why weren't we invited?"

"It was a last-minute affair," Alex said.

"Totally unexpected," Amelia chimed in.

"I see." The twinkle in her eye grew bolder. "Is there a reason for such a rush wedding?"

Amelia looked at Alex. She thought it best for him to tell the strange tale of the wedding. Alex frowned.

"What are you implying?" he asked.

"Should we be airing out the nursery?" the older woman asked. "It will be so nice to have children about the place."

Amelia felt her eyes go wide. Alex gulped and began a coughing fit that had both women pounding him on the back.

"Good Lord, no," he wheezed out. "No need for the nursery. I've only known the gal a couple of days."

The older woman looked confused. "So, then it was love at first sight?"

Amelia thought it was time to step in. It was clear Alex didn't know how best to answer his housekeeper's questions. "It was not love at first sight," she said and tried to sound not the least bit hurt by the idea. "I'm afraid it was all a misunderstanding that got out of hand. Right, Alex?"

"Something like that," Alex said and squeezed her waist. "Mrs. Strasburg, Amelia hasn't seen the entire house. Why don't you take her for a grand tour?"

Amelia turned to him. "I thought—"

"I have some things to do in town." He glanced at his housekeeper. "Don't wait dinner for me." Then he kissed Amelia on the temple and was gone.

She frowned and watched him wind his way through the boxes. "Is he always so abrupt?"

"Only when something is worrying him."

Amelia closed her mouth. She didn't want to speculate on what was worrying Alex. She swallowed the hurt she felt when he said not to hold dinner for him and instead concentrated on the progress she had made. Alex promised that he would not sell Applegate without first giving her father a chance to buy him back.

It was a small thing, but she knew it was a huge concession on Alex's part. She decided to do something nice for him in return. She slipped her arm through Mrs. Strasburg's.

"I would love a grand tour of the house," she said with a brave smile. "Then we can get a cup of tea and talk about all these boxes."

"Oh, you can't touch the boxes," Mrs. Strasburg said. "Mr. Laird gave me specific instructions. The kitchen is the only place I can care for. I guess that makes me just the cook, although I used to be head housekeeper. Still, with not being allowed to keep house, cooking is a fine enough job."

"Well, that might have been before, but he gave me instructions too," she said firmly. "Just now in fact, he told me that I could catalogue all the things in the living areas and then see that they are properly stored."

"Catalogue? Do you know how much he owns, Mrs.?"

Amelia looked around. "We'll begin with his den. That way my husband will have a cozy place to come home to."

*Perhaps he'll want to stay home a little longer, too,* she thought. Then, perhaps, she can do whatever it is that women do to make men fall in love with them.

Alex stayed in town as long as possible, avoiding the beautiful distraction at home. It was the kiss that convinced him he had to leave. She had melted against him, giving him full access to her sweet mouth and soft skin. It had taken every bit of his self-discipline not to sweep her off her feet and take her upstairs to his room. One part of his brain whispered that she was his wife after all, but the rational part reminded him that she would be gone in a few weeks. Unless he did something stupid.

When he got back home, he stayed in the stable for over an hour, doing chores and visiting his animals. Alex looked at his pocket watch. It was well past midnight. He gave Applegate one last handful of oats and closed the stall gate. Glancing around the dark tack room where the cot waited for him, Alex decided he would go up to the house and see if Mrs. Strasburg had left him anything for dessert.

His sweet tooth was acting up and he knew Mrs. Strasburg usually left him a piece of pie in the pie safe for just such emergencies. He wasn't going up to check on Amelia.

The cold wind nearly blew him up the hill to the kitchen door. The darkness around him seemed to laugh at him and he turned up his collar. He was taunted by the fact that he couldn't stay away from his lovely bride. The wind teased him with the notion that somehow, some way his luck had turned. He hadn't won a hand all day.

He wasn't going to blame it on Amelia. It was just a turn of events. Just as the cards left him, they would come back. Lucky at cards, unlucky at love. It was the one constant in his life.

He pushed his hand against the rough oak of the thick kitchen door. The heat of the kitchen enveloped him and he closed the door behind him. Shaking off his coat, he hung it on a peg near the door and walked into the kitchen. The fire had been banked long ago. There was a place setting on the table, and a note.

Alex picked up the paper and read. The note was from Mrs. Strasburg telling him that there were leftovers in the pantry and a pie in the pie safe. It was signed with good night and two cryptic words: "*Your den.*"

Alex crumpled the note and threw it in the wastebasket. What did she mean by his den? What had Amelia done while he was away? His anger rose as he strode through the kitchen, stopping only long enough to light a lamp. He wound his way through the path that was cleared in the dining room, through the central hall and toward his den.

His heartbeat quickened as he swallowed his rising panic. What had happened in his den that made Mrs. Strasburg mention it? He pushed open the door carefully and was surprised to find that it swung open in a wide arc. It had been years since the door opened all the way.

He raised the lamp and stepped inside. The den was half empty. He blinked and glanced around. In the eight or so hours he had been gone, Amelia had managed to move almost half of the mountain of boxes and things he'd stored there. What remained was stacked in pyramid order, biggest to smallest and pushed up against the wall. The cleared space held a wide mahogany desk, complete with a padded leather chair on wheels and a fine gold desk set. Beside the desk was a row of lawyer's bookshelves. They held various volumes on agriculture and estate-keeping. Alex ran his hand over the surface of the shelves. They were freshly polished and smooth as silk. The air was ripe with the scent of bees' wax and something more. There was a hint of femininity among the fragrance of wax, leather and traces of pipe smoke.

He stepped on a thick oriental rug and looked at it. It was freshly beaten, allowing the pattern of deeps reds and greens to blend with the dark leather and mahogany furniture. Across the room the fireplace gleamed. Someone had polished it to within an inch of its life. A noble stag's head graced the wall above it and a soft fire was banked inside, offering a golden glow of heat and light.

Two chairs faced each other in front of the fire. They were sturdy winged back chairs. One had a matching footstool. He caught her sweet scent a moment before he realized that

Amelia sat in one of the winged chairs, fast asleep. She wore an older gown with the sleeves rolled up to her elbows. Wrapped around her was a giant apron that covered every inch of her, and for good reason. It was so soiled that you could hardly see that its true color was white.

Amelia's lovely face was flushed from the heat of the fire. Her thick lashes rested on her pink cheeks. Her sweet mouth was opened slightly. Alex felt himself become calm and quiet inside. It was like happening upon a sleeping fairy. He didn't want to get too close, lest he wake her, but the sight of her was so lovely, he found himself moving forward without a second thought.

She wore a cap that was also no longer white. He knew it was to keep her curls clean, but a few strays had slipped out in protest of their confinement.

Her hands had rolled away from her lap, where a stack of papers and a pencil rested on her apron. Curious, Alex lifted the papers. The pencil rolled off and the slight sound as it hit the rug made Alex jump with guilt.

He glanced at Amelia. She was so exhausted, she slept on. He swallowed and looked down at the papers. They were an inventory of everything she had found thus far in the den.

Alex frowned. He'd forgotten what he had. There was a set of whiskey glasses, a stack of newspapers and newsletters from various gentlemen's organizations. There was the stag's head along with a boar's head, a moose head and buffalo head. Next to the inventory she had written that the other animals were stored in the northern corner of the attic, row 26, boxes seven, eight and nine.

The picture of his attic neat and orderly made him smile. There was nothing neat and orderly about Alex. To be so one had to care and he hadn't cared for years and years.

He gazed at the other five pages of inventory and was shocked by the amount of detail that had gone into cleaning

out just this much of his den. At the end Amelia had penned
a note, probably to herself. The note wondered if there were
any storage facilities in town.

Not that it mattered. What was his, was his for as long as
he kept it. He would never let anyone keep anything that
was his.

He folded the papers and tucked them in his pocket. Then
he set down the lamp on a small side table, walked over to
his orderly bar, and counted five decanters filled with various liquors. They sparkled in the firelight. Beside the
decanters were rows of glasses. Each glass was designed to
showcase a particular drink.

He picked up a brandy glass and poured himself a small
amount. Then he sat down in the chair across from his bride,
put his feet on the footstool and contemplated her. She had
done all this work in the short time he had been gone. He
wondered if she had stopped for dinner and guessed that she
hadn't. If she had, there would be something on the stove
and more work left to be done in the den.

Why had she worked so hard? Why had she picked the den?

He sipped his drink. The answer was obvious. She wanted to please him. No one had ever wanted to please him
before. For a brief moment he felt good, letting hope bright-
en his soul.

Then he took a sip of his brandy and shook the hope away.
In his experience people rarely did anything to please anyone else. There was something she wanted in return for all
this hard work. It was up to him to figure it out.

He contemplated her. She moved, startling him. She did
not wake, but only found a more comfortable spot for her
head. She slipped her hands under her cheek and curled up
her legs. He let go of his cynicism for a moment. Sleeping
there she seemed as innocent and guileless as a child.

He felt a stab of guilt. Of the two, he was the one who

knew better than to wed. He sipped the brandy. He should have stopped their sham of a wedding, but he didn't, and now they were married . . . at least until her father got back.

Until that time he should treat her with the respect that a wife deserved. Which meant, he shouldn't abandon her to her own devices. He glanced around. Who knew what she would do if she set her mind to it?

Alex's thoughts went to the kiss that had sent him rushing madly from the house. She tempted him more than anything ever had, and he didn't know what to do about it.

Abandoning her would be the easy way out. He sipped his brandy and shook his head. He had never taken the easy way out his entire life. That was why he had what he had. In all things he'd been fearless—and that included marrying her. Now he had to figure out how to make things work. Things were out of control because he had no plan of action. He wasn't even in the game.

He had left her to make up the rules as she went along. He glanced around. He did not mind having a usable den, but it was clear he needed to distract her before she found out the extent of his worth. He doubted even Mrs. Strasburg knew exactly what he had in the house. Heck he wasn't too sure himself. He'd lost track of his winnings years ago. To him it was just stuff, but stuff was all he had in his life before Amelia, and stuff would be all he had once Amelia left.

He finished his brandy and got up. Banking the fire, he took a lap blanket off the back of his chair and tucked it in around her. Then because he was compelled, he planted a kiss on her temple.

She sighed and smiled and his heart jumped for a second. He straightened up and shook his head. He told himself not to get caught up in all this domesticity. She would soon be gone and if he weren't careful she'd take more than a dowry with her.

He picked up the lamp and his glass and wandered back to the kitchen. There he left the glass by the sink, pulled on his coat with a sigh, and went out into the cold.

The tack room would be a better place to come up with a plan. If he stayed in the house, he'd be distracted by his own desire and the strong temptation to scoop her up and take her to bed with him.

## Chapter Seven

Amelia awoke in the dead of night. Startled, she sat up and looked around. She was clearly alone in the den, but someone had come in and put a blanket on her. The fire was banked.

She got up and stretched. The den looked so lovely with all the proper things in their proper places. She glanced at the many boxes yet to be gone through and sighed. This project could take years. She had been so excited about clearing this little part of the room that she had taken the time to clean and polish. She wanted Alex to understand what she wanted to do with his house and this was the perfect example.

She looked down and saw that her inventory was missing. Frowning she looked on the desk, but the papers weren't there. She got down on her knees and checked to see that they had not slipped under the chair.

She needed that inventory to prove to Alex that she had kept her promise and kept his stuff. Maybe if he liked what she had done, he wouldn't mind her rearranging more of his things.

There were no papers anywhere on the thick carpet or under the chairs. Puzzled, she sat back on her heels and looked around. Then she heard a noise that made her hold her breath. There was a slight squeak as the door to the den opened. A cold blast of air swirled through the room shooting gooseflesh down her spine. She didn't know whether to declare herself or hide.

Before she could say a word the door closed as quietly as it had opened. She stood up and glanced around. No one had come in. If the fire hadn't given off a spurt from the slight breeze she would have thought she'd made up the whole thing.

Unease came over her like a cold blanket. Was someone sneaking around the house? She stood up and told herself not to be silly. It was simply Mrs. Strasburg checking to see if she went to bed. Or maybe, just maybe it was Alex come home.

"Alex?" she called and went to the door. She opened it and looked out into the dark hallway. "Alex?" Her voice echoed, but not a sound echoed back.

It was as if the whole house held its breath. Amelia wasn't one to take to shivers, but there was something about the darkness that wasn't right.

She ducked back into the den, found a lamp, lit it, and grabbed a heavy poker from beside the fireplace. Then she braved her way out into the hall.

The boxes made it impossible to get a clear view. "Alex, is that you?" she called. "Mrs. Strasburg?" There was no answer. She slipped between the boxes until she came to the juncture where the path split. She could go through the dining room and into the kitchen or she could take the stairs up to her bed.

Amelia bit her lip. A sound came from the dining room. She turned in that direction. "Alex?" She raised her lamp and walked into the room. The rattling of the wind through the windowpanes disturbed the quiet of the old house. She held her breath and listened. Something moved behind her, down the hall.

Spooked, she hurried in the opposite direction to the kitchen. The fire there warmed the room and lent a soft safe glow of light. Her heart pounding, she stopped at the sink and glanced around.

The dishes were put away. The note Mrs. S. had left Alex was wadded up and tossed in the trash making it clear that Alex had come home. She took a deep breath to calm herself. Then she set her lamp down beside the sink and pumped out a fresh cup of clear water.

The water was sweet and soothing to her dry mouth. She shook her head at her own silliness. Alex had probably come in and gone to bed. After all she couldn't expect him to sleep in the stable for the rest of his life.

She tried not to think about where he might be sleeping now. Instead she set the tin cup down beside the sink, picked up her lamp and squaring her shoulders, checked the lock on the back door. It was open.

Amelia shook her head and twisted the bolt shut. Alex had warned her to keep the doors locked. She would have a talk with him in the morning. Her father had taught all of his children from an early age to keep things locked up nice and tidy at night not for the safety of the things in the house, but for the safety of the family.

Her father had seen one too many Indian raids. Now Amelia couldn't sleep without at least one locked door between her and the dark forest outside.

She picked up her lamp, adjusted the wick and decided to go to bed. In the morning she would have that talk with Alex and when she did, she'd also chastise him for scaring the bejebbers out of her by sneaking through the house and not answering when she called.

It was something her brothers would do on dark nights at home. They would sneak through the house, hide behind curtains, then pop out at unsuspecting passersby. It was enough to make you jump right out of your skin. Of course, the boys found it all hilarious. Well, Amelia wasn't going to put up with that.

If Alex persisted with these silly schoolboy shenanigans, then she would have to come up with something equally as clever with which to retaliate.

That thought kept her focused and brave as she made her way up to her bedroom. She opened the door and was a little disappointed to find that Alex wasn't there.

She had no idea what she would have done had he been there. Probably climbed into bed right beside him. The thought made her heart pound and butterflies kick up in her stomach. Sleeping next to a man would surely count as keeping in close proximity. Maybe she needed to move that up in importance on her list perhaps to number two, right after looking and smelling good. After all, if a man stayed close then you could actually try your hand at cooking and agreeing with him.

She set the lamp down on her dresser and took out her nightgown. Her reflection frowned back at her. She had spent the day organizing his den. Something she loved to do, but not something on her redemption list.

She shook her head at herself. She had let him distract her from her cause. That was not good. She changed into her bedclothes, pulled the cap off her head and unwound her long hair. Then she sat down and began the ritual 100 brush strokes before bed.

As she stroked, she made a plan for the next day. She

would start with Applegate and a quick ride. Then she would hunt down her husband and have a talk with him about keeping the doors locked. Then she would go in search of the library he claimed to have.

Perhaps she would get lucky and he would have a book on the finer points of falling in love. She bit her lip and put down her brush. If it had been Alex who put the blanket on her in the den, then he had seen her looking like a maidservant.

She had broken yet another rule.

Braiding her hair, Amelia rolled her eyes at herself. Getting a man to fall in love with you was much harder than she had ever imagined. If only her sisters were here to help. She twisted a ribbon around the end of her waist-long hair and got up. She poured water from the pitcher into the basin and washed her face and hands.

A moment later she pulled back the covers and climbed into bed. The linens were cool and smelled of fresh air. She blew out her lamp and snuggled under the covers. As she drifted off she tried to imagine what it would be like if Alex's head rested beside her own.

Alex checked to make sure he was alone before he dunked his head into the basin of cold water. The shock of it hit him clear to his toes. He shook his head, flinging water around the tack room. Then he grabbed a towel, wiped off his face and slicked back his hair as usual. He reached for his shirt and pulled it over his head.

The tack room was cool and dim in the morning light. Again he hadn't gotten a whole lot of sleep because he had laid awake on the stiff cot picturing Amelia's sweet face. She had cleaned up his den and organized his belongings. It was the nicest thing anyone had ever done for him.

Besides that, he found himself drawn to her—the sparkle in her eyes, the innocence of her smile, the way she watched him, quiet and contemplative as if she could see into his soul.

"Yeah, right." He slammed his feet into his boots. Today he'd go into town and have a good long bath and a shave. Then after a fine meal at Millie's he'd have a successful afternoon of card play. That was his plan.

He stepped outside the tack room and walked over to Applegate's stall and clicked his tongue. Cold silence answered him. A serious dread ran down his spine. He ripped open the stall door.

The prize animal was gone. Darn it! She had lulled him with her organizing. Then as soon as she could, she'd stolen the horse and run off.

He grabbed his saddle, pulled out his best gelding, saddled the horse, and quickly mounted. If she thought she could run away from him, she had another think coming.

He left the stable at a run, taking off down the long winding drive toward the gate. The woods opened up and he had a view of pastures to the west. He saw her in the distance.

The sight took his breath away. He rose up on his toes in his stirrups and took it all in. Amelia and Applegate rode on the wind. The horse and rider blurred across the field. They galloped at breakneck speed, leaping across streams and fences.

It was as if they were on a suicide mission. Alex frowned and observed their direction, then did some quick figuring. He clicked his tongue and pushed his horse off the drive. Keeping Amelia and Applegate in the corner of his eye, Alex took a short cut around them, down one hill and up the next.

He sat on the rise and waited for her to ride toward him. She didn't disappoint him. If Applegate were a runaway, he would help her, if not, he was going to have a talk with her about risking both his horse and her neck.

At the calculated moment, he kicked his animal into a

dead run, down the hill. Amelia didn't see him until he was nearly upon her. Her startled glance told him more than words. She was racing and she never expected anyone else to keep up.

"Slow down," he shouted.

She grinned at him and clung to the reins.

"I said slow down."

"Make me," she dared him and spurred ahead.

Anger, excitement, anticipation shot through him and he spurred his mount into action. He would catch her all right, not just because he was a better rider, but also because he knew the land.

He flew over a low stone wall and cut around a small clearing of trees. There was a hill coming up. That would slow her some along with the stream she'd have to leap at the bottom.

His heart raced, his muscles strained as he urged his horse forward. The wind was cold and fresh against his face. He drew closer to her just when he thought he would. Applegate hesitated over the stream. It was a small, barely discernable movement, but it was enough to help him catch up.

Her petticoats flew even with his knee. She glanced at him. Her laughing eyes sparkled as she grinned and urged her mount on up the hill.

Alex made sure that he had the most ideal path up the hill. The stallion was strong and took the rockier path well. Still he was able to reach for her reins just as they cleared the top. He pulled both animals to a halt.

The sun rose strong and red over the edge of the world. The air was full of mist from their combined breath and the heavy huffing of the animals. Applegate tossed his head in protest.

"Whoa," Amelia said and patted her horse's neck. "Whoa,

baby." She glanced at Alex. The look seared through him, straight to his heart. She grinned again that happy, carefree smile that made her sparkle. "You won."

He held up the reins. "I won." The moment was so bright and clear and exhilarating that he bent down and kissed her fully on the mouth. Instead of pulling away, she reached up and wrapped her arms around his neck and kissed him back.

Caught off guard by the enthusiasm of her kiss, he found himself being pulled off the horse. He broke off the kiss, hopped down and pulled her down with him.

She was so alive in his arms. Her breath was ragged from the ride and she gasped as he pulled her against him. His heart raced, his blood warmed and he felt so wonderfully alive. More alive than he'd felt in years.

He wrapped his hands around her waist and drew her to him. She smiled at him and reached up to plant small kisses on his cheeks. "Great race," she said. "Next time, I won't let you win."

"What?!"

She pulled away from him, careful to take Applegate's reins from his hand. "I said nice race."

"I heard that part," he said and took hold of Applegate's bridle. The stallion tried to toss his head, but Alex was strong enough to hold him. "It's the other part I'm disagreeing with."

"What part?" she asked all wide-eyed and innocent. He knew better, but still the flirtation was fun. He reached out and brushed a wayward curl from her face.

"The part where you claim to have thrown the race." He lifted the curl to his lips and kissed it. Then let his gaze go to her lips.

Her mouth opened in a surprised little, "Oh."

It was such an innocent thing but it had him wanting

things he hadn't dreamed of in years—things from fairy tales about love and happily-ever-afters.

The shock ran clear through him. He let her hair slip out of his fingers and took a step forward. She retreated against the horse. "I did throw the race."

"No, you didn't," he said. "I calculated this win."

"That's what I wanted you to think."

"That's what happened." He took another step toward her.

"You keep believing that," she said, stepping away. "I'm sure it makes you feel better."

"Why, you little . . ." He took off after her.

She giggled and raced across the top of the hill. Breathless, he ran after her. Intent on his prey, he hunted her down. She stopped and held onto a tree, trying to keep it between them.

He let her feel confident for a moment, then snaked around and caught her by the waist. She squealed and protested, just enough to make it worthwhile catching her.

Then he kissed her. The kiss was sweeter than the finest candy. It drew out dreams and wishes and all that was once the child inside him. Things he'd thought long gone.

He broke off the kiss and studied her. She blinked up at him. They were both breathing hard. Somewhere a bird called. The wind rushed passed them toward the lake in the distance. A lone autumn leaf swirled past.

He ran his fingers along her cheek. Her skin was soft and warm with a flush so pink it was like cotton candy against the blue sky. With her dark blue eyes full of possibilities, her flushed alabaster skin and silky hair, she looked like dawn.

Wanting was something he couldn't indulge himself—neither were kisses and flirting—if not for his sake, then for hers.

"Alex?"

He drew back his fingers and turned to gather the horses. "Alex?"

"Don't ever do that again," he said and struggled to get his emotions under wraps. She was not his, at least not for long.

"Do what? My riding? I'm a good rider, Alex. I've been riding Applegate like that since he was first trained. I haven't broken my neck yet."

"It's not your neck I'm worried about."

"Applegate loves to run. I swear he was in no danger."

Alex turned on her. "And when he steps in a gopher hole and breaks his leg, what will you do? Hmm? How will you pay me for the animal you abused?"

"I would never abuse Applegate!"

"Running him across unknown territory is abuse," he said. "Until you've both been here long enough to know every nook and cranny of the place I suggest you keep your riding to a more sedate pace."

She put her hands on her hips and stomped her foot at him. "I will ride my horse any way I want."

"You will ride *my* horse with care and the respect due him," Alex said and mounted. He looked down at her. She nearly had steam coming from her ears. Just to get her goat he added, "Restraint is the mark of good breeding."

She gasped. "I'm restrained."

"Honey, right now this stallion shows more restraint than you." As if to mock her, Applegate shook his head and rolled his eyes.

Alex watched her jaw drop and had to work to hide his amusement. He reached down and offered her his hand. "Come on, let's go home."

"I'll ride Applegate," she said and grabbed the edge of his saddle. She mounted the horse as gracefully as a queen takes her throne. "I promise, we won't outrun you."

Alex reached over and grabbed the stallion's reins. "I told you I don't want him to race."

"You'll break his spirit."

"It's for his own good," Alex said with pointed meaning.

"Applegate isn't the kind of horse that should be reined in."

"Let me ask you this, what would your father have said if he'd seen you racing hell bent for leather over unknown fields?"

She sat up straight. "He would have been proud."

"He would have banished you from riding for a week."

"You don't know my father."

"No, I don't, but I do know horses and any man who would let you put this stallion in jeopardy isn't a man I want to know."

That seemed to get through to her. She snapped her mouth shut and let him lead her down the slope. Alex breathed a sigh of relief. She really needed a keeper. The worst part was, he wanted to volunteer for the job.

Her energy and enthusiasm had brought excitement back to his life. Everything she did was heartfelt and headfirst. Even the way she kissed him. It made him wonder what other things she might do with such abandon.


He left her at the kitchen door with the stern admonishment not to ride Applegate again without his permission. She wanted to kick him. Really she did. The man had no sense of fair play.

She turned and stormed into the kitchen. Okay, so he was right, her father would have had a fit if he'd seen her running Applegate like that. She had always made a point of doing it where he couldn't see.

It seemed she'd have to take the same tack when it came to her husband. Really, they had no idea how good Applegate was. He would never do something as silly as break a leg in a foxhole. Besides, she was too good a rider to let him.

"Did you have a good ride?" Mrs. Strasburg asked.

Amelia went over to the sink and washed her hands. "I

think I made Alex mad," she admitted and dried her hands on the towel that hung from the stove handle. "At least I got his attention."

"Oh, you have his attention," the older woman said with a smile.

Amelia shook her head. "Not in a good way." She sat down at the table where Mrs. Strasburg kneaded bread dough. "Can I ask you a question?"

"Sure."

"Do you think I'm unrestrained?"

"Are you asking me if I think you're a tomboy?"

"I guess." She brushed the hair out of her face. "Do I truly seem unpolished to you?"

"Well," the older woman said, "I wouldn't say you were a tomboy. No, I'd say you were simply . . . enthusiastic."

"I see." She traced markings in the floured table surface with a wooden spoon handle. "Do you think men prefer a wife who is more sedate?"

Mrs. Strasburg laughed. "It depends on the man. My Bert loves a little laughter now and then. An occasional show of emotion goes a long way to spicing up life."

Amelia thought about that for a while. "Do you think Alex likes a restrained woman?"

"Hard to tell. He's never brought a woman home before, so I really have no idea what kind of woman he prefers." She glanced at Amelia. "Since he brought you home, I'm thinking that perhaps you are the kind of woman he prefers."

Amelia bit her tongue. It wouldn't do to blurt out the truth. No, it was better for Alex's servants to believe that he married her over something more than a dare.

"I do want to thank you again for helping me so long last night. Why if not for you and Mr. S I would never have gotten the den looking as nice as it does."

"I should have a few hours again today if you want to do

more," the cook said with enthusiasm. "You have no idea how long I've wanted to get at it."

"We'll see," Amelia said. "It might be better if we ease Alex into the idea of a comfortable home. I think we should work a couple more days in the den. I want you to think about what room we should do after that."

"Oh, there's no thinking to be done," Mrs. Strasburg said. "I'd love to have a dining room people could actually eat in."

"Good, then we'll do that next." Amelia stood up. "I'm going to change out of these riding clothes. Then if you don't mind, I think I'm going to see if I can't find that library Alex told me he had."

"The library is the first right, just past the conservatory," Mrs. Strasburg said with a friendly shake of her head. "Good luck finding the floor in there."

Amelia smiled. "Perhaps, after the dining room, the library is the next room to inventory, hmm?"

So, Alex thought she was unrestrained. Well, she'd show him how unrestrained she could be. She'd simply keep cleaning away until she had his whole house sorted. She wondered what he'd think of that? Then again perhaps she didn't care what he thought. It would be interesting just to see exactly what her husband had "collected" over the years. If yesterday was any indication, it was certainly going to be interesting. She whistled to herself and hurried up the stairs.

## Chapter Eight

Mrs. Strasburg had been right about the library. When Amelia first forced the door open enough to squeeze in, she found it packed floor to ceiling. Mrs. Strasburg told her Alex had once won the contents of a freighter that had just made its way from the orient. The ship's captain was so angry that he had given Alex only two days to unload the hold. Alex had hired fifteen men and several wagons the contents of which currently resided unopened in the library.

It took Amelia the rest of the day to sort her way through the library. She had no clue how she was supposed to find a book in there. She had never seen so many bolts of silk, pieces of china and brass. There were three barrels of various spices, which she had Mr. Strasburg take to the cellar right away. Mrs. Strasburg smiled.

"We always check the house before we go shopping," she said. "Truthfully, we are more likely to find what we need stuffed somewhere."

Amelia laughed. "The man is obsessive."

"This is his life."

"It's just stuff," she said. "Stuff he should sell so that someone can get some use out of it."

"It might be stuff to you, but it's all he has," Mrs. Strasburg said. Then she walked back to the kitchen and left Amelia to ponder what that meant.

Later that evening, Amelia sat on an old leather chair and looked around the library. The boxes were pushed to the center and restacked. What remained were four walls of books stacked floor to ceiling. There were more books than Amelia had ever seen in her entire life. The best part was they were already set up in alphabetical order by author.

There was a wonderful old ladder that rolled along the wall so that the books on the top shelf could be reached as easily as the books near the bottom. She had gone through a small number of the volumes dusting the shelves, when she came upon a most interesting book.

*The Art of Taking a Lover* by Mort Viarite. Amelia had pulled the book off the shelf and stuffed it in her apron pocket. Lighting a lantern to hold back the dimming light at the end of the day, she settled into the chair and opened the tome.

It started with a small forward by a Lady Chamberlain who wanted to insist that the secrets inside were meant for married women only. Amelia nodded. She was married.

The book was educating. At one point Mrs. Strasburg stuck her head into the library to tell Amelia that she was leaving dinner on the stove. Amelia blushed at being caught reading the book, but thought she concealed it well when she waved out the older woman.

The book was quite risqué, explaining to Amelia things she had never considered. Like the fact that the marriage bed was about more than sleeping and how a man could be intimate with a woman in over a hundred different ways.

Some of the illustrations were enlightening, although she was certain that human beings simply didn't bend that way.

A noise down the hall made her jump. She looked up to see that it had become completely dark outside. The wind kicked up, brushing the bushes against the windows and howling. She glanced at the watch pinned to her chest. It was nearly ten o'clock. She figured that Alex came in for dinner at night around eleven. Perhaps that was what she heard down the hall.

She shut the book quickly, with a tinge of guilt. The last thing she wanted was for Alex to know she would read such a book. Her father would have a fit if he knew.

She slipped the book into her pocket. It crumpled against some paper. She pulled out her list of how to make a man fall in love. She laughed at herself. The list now seemed sadly lacking. In the morning there were things that needed to be added—things she had no idea how to put on a list.

A door opened and banged closed somewhere out in the hallway. She folded the paper neatly and slipped it back into her pocket behind the book. Then she smoothed the ruffled edges of her apron and ran a hand over her hair to smooth it as well. It didn't slow her quickened heart.

Alex was home. She would feed him dinner and try some of the small seductions described in chapter two of the book. Her stomach fluttered at the idea. What if she were successful? If they got as far as chapter nine she would be completely and totally out of the realm of her imagination. Was she brave enough to get there?

The answer was yes. Determined, she raised her chin and stood up. The book guaranteed that a man would find a woman who did those things completely irresistible.

She took a deep breath and settled herself. Alex was her husband and he deserved a good wife. It was up to her to make herself irresistible.

She looked down. She was still dressed for cleaning. Stupid. She should have gone upstairs and changed into her best gown. Why couldn't she remember rule number one? Always show your husband your best side.

She sighed when she heard another door open and close. She didn't have time to change. She took off her apron and stuffed it under the chair cushion. It was now or never.

She opened the door. The hallway was dark and drafty, and very much empty of life. "Alex?" she called. When there was no answer, she grabbed her lamp and walked out to the conservatory. "Alex, I'm in the conservatory. Are you ready for dinner?"

Shadows danced against the glass, slipping in and out of the stacks of boxes and furniture covered in sheets. "Alex? This is not funny, please show yourself."

There was a skitter of footsteps and a far door opened and closed. Amelia was getting angry. How many nights would he do this to her? It was frightening and insulting.

"Alex. I said stop it. I know you're home. Now come out, we need to talk." Silence met her request. She raised the lamp so that the circle of light included most of the path through the room. "Alex?"

She edged around a set of boxes to see that he had been going through the boxes. "Alex?" Things were strewn about. In fact it appeared that he had only looked through the boxes, lifting out lamps and trinkets and scattering them about, as if he were looking for something but had not found it.

"I can inventory this room for you next if you'd like . . . Alex?"

She thought she heard breathing and whirled toward the far end of the room. A black shadow turned and slipped through the boxes. Her heart raced when it crossed her mind that perhaps it wasn't Alex in the room with her.

Amelia picked up a silver candelabrum and held it like a

weapon in her left hand while she lifted the light from the lamp in her right. "Who's there? Declare yourself."

There was a loud bang and she jumped. Amelia bit her lip and stepped toward the shadows. "Come out now, I've got you." The light shone into the darkness. She rounded a corner of boxes and gasped, holding back a scream.

Standing there was a man. In an instant, she knew one thing. It wasn't Alex. She swung the candelabra. It connected with the man's head knocking it clean off. A metallic thud echoed through the surrounding darkness. "Good Lord!" She lifted the lantern to see that she had beheaded a suit of armor. "Right," she said under her breath and tried to calm herself. Just for good measure she kicked the suit. "Stupid thing nearly scared me half to death."

"Is that how you treat a knight in shining armor?"

This time she did scream and whirled to see Alex leaning against the nearest pile of boxes.

"Didn't know I looked that bad," he said and straightened.

Amelia put her hand on her chest. "You have scared me half to death." Just for good measure she stormed up and smacked his arm. "It's not funny," she said, tears welling up. "You will stop this madness."

"What madness? Coming home?"

"No, purposely scaring me. If you don't want me here, just say so. Don't try to scare me off."

He reached out and pulled her against him. "I'm not trying to scare you off." He tucked her head against his chest. He was big and warm and real, but she was so upset she refused to lean into him.

"Yes, you are. Every night since I came here, you've tried to scare me."

"I have not."

"Yes, you have," she said and pulled away from him. "I hear you skulking about the hallways. The first night I locked my door. Last night I followed you into the kitchen, but you refused to answer me. Then tonight—"

"Tonight I heard a noise and came to investigate."

"No, I heard you in the hallway. I followed you into this room. I called your name but you refused to answer me."

He tugged her back against him, a frown forming on his handsome face. "I just came into this room when I heard the rattling of armor."

"No, I saw you run between these boxes."

"It wasn't me."

His words sent a chill down her spine. "Mr. Strasburg?"

"They went to bed hours ago."

"Then who?"

"I don't know, but I think it's time I found out." He took the lantern from her hand. "Where did you see this person go?"

"That way," she said and pointed toward the dark corner.

"If I remember right, there's a door there, out to the gardens."

"Do you think he's gone?" she whispered.

"I think I need to check the locks." He stepped around the remnants of the suit of armor. "Stay here."

"No, I'm going with you," she said and grabbed the back of his jacket. "I've had enough of being all by myself."

He didn't argue. Instead he headed down the winding isle of boxes. The darkness enveloped them, shooting shadows off the boxes and various things piled head high. Finally, they reached the wall. A set of glass doors creaked open and shut with the wind. The draperies blew in and out as if a giant monster were breathing in wild gusts. She felt the hair on her arms stand up.

"The lock's been busted," Alex said. He handed her the lantern and closed the doors. Then he dug around until he found a long metal rod and jammed it between the door handles. "That should keep him out until morning."

"How many doors are in this house?" she asked.

"More than I'm comfortable with," he said grimly and took the lantern. "I think I'll have a walk around and see that they are all locked."

"That's a good idea," she said and wrapped her arms around her waist.

"You're shaking."

"It's a bit startling to think that strangers have been in the house."

He put his arm around her and drew her against him. His frown had deepened with the shadows. "Come on. Let's get you a cup of tea."

She grabbed him. "You aren't going to leave me, are you?"

"Just long enough to check the doors," he said. "No sense in both of us wandering through the entire house at this time of night."

"Oh, yes there is," she said firmly. "What if he's still in the house? What if he attacks you?"

"That's not going to happen."

"I'm not willing to take that chance," she said stubbornly. "I'm not going to wait in the kitchen with a cup of tea while some intruder attacks you and leaves you dying. It could be a week before I find you in this massive old place."

He smiled with an odd lift of one corner of his mouth. His grip tightened on her. "No one's ever worried about me before."

"You've never been married before," she answered simply. "It's a wife's job to worry about her husband. That's what love is all about."

"Really?" He shook his head. "I thought wives worried because of the income they would lose when their husbands died."

"You are a terrible cynic," she said. Her heart ached with

sadness for him. She reached up and caressed his cheek. "How did you get to be so?"

"Experience," he said gravely and pushed her hand away.

"Someday you will tell me who hurt you so badly."

"No one hurt me," he said. "Come on. We've got doors to check and it's getting late."

"Alex?"

"What?"

"Would you worry about me?"

"What do you mean?"

"I mean if whoever broke into the house had taken me, would you worry?"

He glanced at her. "Of course."

"Why?"

"Because you're my wife."

"But I don't bring you any income."

"No, you don't."

"Still you would worry."

"Yes."

"Why?"

"I don't know. Honor, I guess."

"Honor?"

"Yes, honor. I took those vows of my free will." He headed out of the room. "I'll keep them."

"You're a good man, Alex Laird."

"Right." They proceeded in silence to check all twelve doors in the jam-packed mansion.

"If you sleep out in the stables, then I'm going with you."

A small part of Alex liked the idea. The cot in the tack room was very narrow. The idea of holding Amelia close through the night was appealing, too appealing for his peace of mind. Yet she was right. He couldn't leave her alone in the house anymore. Not after what he'd seen tonight.

Someone had made a habit of visiting at night. The darn house was so big and packed with stuff that he hadn't even noticed. It was time to change all that.

"What bedroom are you sleeping in?"

"What?" she squeaked.

Now that was an interesting reaction. He glanced over at her and raised an eyebrow. "What room are you sleeping in?"

She put the small stack of plates down on the table. He could tell she was gathering her nerve. "I'm sleeping in the east wing. The second bedroom on the left."

"The blue room."

"Yes." She set the table pretending to be nonchalant but he could tell she was nervous. He leaned against the counter and wondered what she was thinking.

"Good choice."

"Thank you. I thought the view was lovely."

"It's the best bed in the place."

She glanced up at him, concern on her face. "Oh, was it your room?"

He let a slight smile cross his face and pushed off the counter. "No." He turned and lifted the lid on the pot of venison soup Mrs. Strasburg had left simmering on the stove.

"Then how do you know?"

"About what?" He ladled soup into a tureen.

"How do you know it has the best bed?"

"There are ten bedrooms in the place," he said as he put the soup on the table. "I checked them all out."

"I see." She clutched the top of her chair. "I suppose as owner it's important to know the lay of the land."

"Exactly," he said and gathered up a loaf of fresh bread and a plate of butter. He put them on the table. Then he eased her chair out of her hands and pulled it out for her. "After you."

She sat and let him push her in. Then he sat, taking the napkin out of its holder, he put it on his lap and ladled out soup.

"I'm curious," she said.

"About?"

"Well, if the best bed is in my room, why don't you sleep in it?"

"Is that an invitation?"

She blushed a becoming pink. "It's common sense," she said, and put her energy into cutting a slice of bread.

"I like the room at the top of the stairs. It's bigger and has access to the main parts of the house."

She buttered a piece of her bread. "Well, then why didn't you simply move the best bed into that room?" She slipped the bread into her mouth.

That little action made his stomach clench. He couldn't take his eyes off the small bit of butter that clung to the edge of her mouth. It made her lips shiny and he remembered how she tasted.

"Alex?"

"Hmm?"

"Why didn't you move the bed?"

"Move the bed?"

"Yes, I'm sure you and Mr. Strasburg could easily have handled moving the bed from my room to yours."

Alex looked down at his soup and shrugged. "I didn't think I'd be here long enough for it to matter." He spooned up some of the soup. It was warm and salty, bursting with flavor. "I suppose we could move the bed in the morning." He glanced at her. "But then where would you sleep?"

"You have ten bedrooms, silly," she said with a sigh. "It would be nothing to move into another room."

He had to work hard at not inviting her to sleep with him.

The way he figured, they had only a few more days before her father would be knocking down the gate to get her back.

She was lovely and tempting but as he had said earlier, he was a man of honor. It was his honor that kept him in control. It was better this way. She would have an annulment and he would have the horse with no harm done except maybe to his wayward heart.

He pushed away the thought that the house would be horribly empty once she left. But it had been empty before. He'd get used to it being empty again.

"May I ask you a personal question?" she asked between spoonfuls of soup.

"Sure."

"What do you do all day?"

"I play cards," he said. "It's what I do, Amelia. I'm a gambler."

"So, you go into town and gamble."

"Yes."

"Why? I mean with all you own, you could be a farmer. Why, you could afford to be a gentleman farmer with workers and a manager. With Applegate and the mares I saw in your stable you could be a horse breeder."

"I could be, but I'm not."

"Why not?"

"Look," he said and pushed away from the table. "I am what you see. A gambler. That's it. That's who you married. I don't see any reason to try to be what I'm not."

She put her elbows on the table and rested her chin in her hands. "How do you know what you're not? Have you ever tried to be a farmer?"

"No."

"Have you ever tried to be a horse breeder?"

"No."

"Then how do you know that you're not these things?"

He put his dishes in the sink then turned to lean against the counter. He crossed his arms over his chest. "Does it disappoint you to be married to a gambler?"

"If you're asking me if I'm disappointed being married to you, the answer is no." She leaned back in her chair and contemplated him. "If you're a gambler because that's what makes you happy, then I'm satisfied with that. Are you happy, Alex?"

"What's happiness?"

"I don't know." She shrugged. "Having a dream, I think. People need to chase the dreams that are in their hearts. I think that's how they become happy."

"What is your dream?"

"Me?" She laughed and picked up her dishes. He stepped aside as she brushed past him to place her dishes in the sink.

"Yes, you, Amelia." He took a deep breath and drew in the sweet candy scent of her skin. "What is your dream?"

"I always dreamed of raising horses," she said softly. She turned and stood mere inches from him. "It's why Applegate is so important to me. I want to pick his mares and see his children and his grandchildren born. I want to start a dynasty of horses so grand that the entire world will come knocking on our door simply to watch our horses play in the fields. That's my dream, Alex. That's why I'm content to be married to you." She reached up and touched his cheek. "You have everything I ever wanted, Applegate, this lovely estate. Absolutely everything."

Guilt engulfed him. Her wide eyes shone with truth. All he wanted was the horse and the only reason he wanted it was because he won it. Unlike her, he had no grand plan. Life was too unpredictable for that.

"I'm not a breeder, Amelia." He hated to erase the dream

from her eyes but the truth was all he really had. "The truth is I'm a gambler and I could lose this estate and Applegate." He stepped away from the temptation of the dream in her eyes. "This time next year you may be married to a man with no home and no wealth."

She stepped toward him, surprising him. "That's a gamble I'm willing to take. You see, Alex, I see so much more in you. When you look at yourself, all you see is deuces. I see aces or better yet, a solid chance at a royal flush."

"Then you are a fool."

"Far from it," she said with confidence in her voice. "I'm simply not afraid. You see I have a secret."

"You do?"

"Yes."

"Care to share?"

She smiled a secret smile. "I'm a very good gambler. In fact, I bet I'm better than you."

Now that was a challenge a man could not pass up. He wrapped his hands around her arms and drew her to him. "No one is better than me, Amelia." He kissed her on that sassy mouth.

It brought a sweet rush through his blood. Her skin was soft and warm. Her mouth hungry and challenging. She melted against him in a slow slide of soft cotton, satiny lace and the heat of a willing woman.

Something deep inside him cracked. He allowed himself this brief moment to want. It was something he hadn't ever allowed himself to feel, for wanting meant having and having always led to losing.

She slid her hands up his shoulders, then her fingers through his hair. He wanted to lose himself in her confidence. To dream for even the briefest of seconds of having this place forever, of watching their horses grow, of watching their children grow, of leaving a legacy far greater than that of a legendary gambler. The dream was as sweet a temptation as her taste upon his lips.

She pulled back and caught her breath. "Okay," she said with agreement. "So, you are very good, but I'm still better."

He laughed at her then. That sweet innocence, believing she could conquer the world. "Care to make a bet on that?"

"Sure," she said and licked her lips. The motion nearly brought him to his knees.

"What do you have to offer?"

"What do you have to lose?"

The question had the hair on the back of his neck rising. "It seems that I have more to lose than you have to offer."

"Perhaps," she said with that secret smile. "But then I thought you were certain you would win. If that's true you wouldn't be afraid to bet it all."

It was his turn to laugh. "And what do you have that is worth all this?"

She looked at him with deep sincere eyes. "My love."

Sweat sprung up on his palms and he stepped away. "What if I'm not looking for your love?"

"Not even unconditional love? Come on, Alex, that is one thing I know you don't have."

He turned his back on her. The temptation was overwhelming. *Unconditional love. What would that be like? Is it possible to have it?* For one brief moment he tried to wrap his mind around the idea. A picture of her looking at him, her eyes filled with love. In his mind they were both old and gray and still she looked at him as if she could never stop loving him, as if he had never disappointed, as if she had the sure and certain knowledge that they would go to their graves without ever disappointing each other.

He turned to see what she offered and the temptation of

that dream was more than he could resist. "Fine. I would have your unconditional love. That means that you will love me even if I lose this house, and all these things I have."

"Of course."

"You will love me even if I sell Applegate."

She simply smiled. "Even if you sell Applegate."

"You would love me when I'm old and fat."

Her smile deepened. "Even then."

"And what will you want if you win this bet?"

"That's simple. I want you to become a breeder of fine horses and a gentleman farmer."

He made a face. "I'd be terrible at it."

"You won't know that until you try."

"I'd have thought you'd ask for something tangible like Applegate or this house and the things inside it."

"I know."

"What do you know?"

"I know that you expect so little of people that you would expect me to want to win the material things you own." She touched him, her hand a warm caress on his arm. "I don't care about that," she said solemnly. "What I care about is our future and that isn't found in material things."

He studied her a moment in silence, then shrugged. It didn't matter, she wasn't going to win. He was the best card player in three states.

"You're on."

"Good," she stepped away. "I'll go get some cards."

He watched her walk away and wondered at the way women thought. The way he figured, in just a matter of an hour or so Applegate would be his completely. When her father came for her, she would have to relinquish the horse. It would be part of the bargain of unconditional love.

His heart squeezed. He knew that love was not something

you could win, but rather something freely given. At least he imagined it worked that way. For no one had ever freely given him anything. Therefore love was to him the same as smoke, barely visible in the air. Something that can never be touched. Something that would disappear in a stiff wind.

## Chapter Nine

"What is going on here?" Mrs. Strasburg asked as she walked into the kitchen.

"A very good game of cards," Amelia answered the cook. She eyed her cards, then bet a series of matchsticks. It had been decided that the stakes would be a box of wooden matches. The first person to win all of the sticks would be the official winner of the bet.

Alex played aggressively, but she was slowly and steadily beating him. Right now, she had half his matchsticks and from the look on his face much more of his respect.

"It's six o'clock in the morning," Mrs. Strasburg said and rolled up her sleeves. "When did you start this game?"

"Last night," Alex replied and matched Amelia's bet. "How many?" he asked her, picking up the stack of dealer's cards.

"Three please."

He raised an eyebrow at her. They each had five cards and she had put down a significant bet. "Three for the clever lady," he muttered.

Amelia tossed out three cards and pulled in the new.

"I'll take two," he said and dealt himself two new cards.

"So neither of you has had any sleep," the cook said rattling around filling the coffeepot with water and grinding coffee beans. She lit the stove and boiled the brew. "I suppose I'll have to make more than one pot of coffee."

Amelia smiled. She really liked the older woman. It was like having a mother-figure around. Something she barely remembered but had often longed for. She glanced down at her new cards. Alex had dealt her an ace, a jack and a queen in the suit she already had in her hand. She had a straight flush.

She pushed in ten more sticks. "I'll add to the bet." She watched Alex as he frowned at his cards. It was clear he was uncertain what to do.

Luck rewarded the daring. For Amelia, what had started out as a bluff had turned into something much better. Amelia smiled when it hit her that it was the same with her marriage.

"You're bluffing," Alex groused.

"Am I?"

"Yes." He raised a dark eyebrow and sent her a smile that made her knees go weak. "I'm calling you." He put in the extra sticks.

"I figured you would," she said and laid down her cards. "Flush."

His face fell. "I have no idea how you do it," he muttered and put down his cards. He had a pair of queens and a pair of twos.

She scooped up the pot and added it to her pile.

"Why don't you two put away the game and have some breakfast?" Mrs. Strasburg asked as she set hot cups of coffee in front of them. "Pancakes will be done soon."

"Alex doesn't eat breakfast," Amelia said and sipped the coffee. She hadn't realized how tired she was until she smelled the coffee and her body told her brain that she had been up all night.

"Pancakes will be fine," Alex said and picked up the cards. He shuffled them absently between his long fingers.

Amelia yawned, careful to cover her mouth. "Oh, my," she said. "Excuse me."

"Perhaps Mrs. Strasburg is right. We should continue this later tonight."

"Are you hoping time will change your luck?" Amelia challenged him. "Or are you planning on stealing some of my matchsticks?"

"Neither," he said and set the cards aside. He stretched. The long lean line of muscle moving under his shirt made her catch her breath. "I think it's a good time to look around and see exactly what our intruder has been up to."

"What intruder?" Mrs. Strasburg asked as she poured pancake batter into hot cast-iron pans.

"Someone's been in the house at night," Amelia said.

"What?! Why didn't you say anything?"

"I thought it was Alex."

"But it wasn't," Alex said. "Best I can tell whoever is coming in has been doing the same thing Amelia has been doing, taking stock of what I own."

"That's not fair," she said. It hurt to hear him say it like that. It sounded as if he thought she was greedy and wanted to know exactly what they owned. "I don't care what you have in those rooms. What I care about is being able to live in this great big storage barn of a house."

Incensed, she stood up. "If it bothers you so much, I'll limit my cleaning activities to my room." She picked up her skirts. "Now, if you'll excuse me, I'm tired and I'm going to bed."

He stopped her by grabbing her arm as she passed by. "I

didn't mean to insult you." His voice was low and soothing, his dark eyes filled with an emotion that felt like a deep caress. "Stay and have breakfast with me."

"As lovely as breakfast sounds, I'm going to have to decline." She glanced at the older woman who was stacking fluffy pancakes on plates. "Please wake me at noon. I've so much to do and I need to be at least a little rested or I'll not think clearly."

"I'll do that," Mrs. Strasburg said and put the pancakes on the table.

Amelia's gaze followed her to the table and she realized she was so tired, she had nearly left her stack of matches on the table. She reached over and slid them into both hands. "No cheating."

"I don't need to cheat."

"You've never played me before," she said with all the confidence inside her. He simply raised his eyebrows.

"That's a lot of confidence for a woman."

"My confidence doesn't come from being a woman, Alex. It comes from my skill." She raised her hands to show off how they bulged with matchsticks. "Be prepared to start a new career."

"You should be prepared to give up that horse," he said. "When I win, I'm thinking of selling the stallion."

She swallowed the spike of doubt that ran through her. "If you win, my father will be happy to buy him. Good day, Alex." She forced herself to sail out of the kitchen.

Making her way through the path of boxes she dismissed the dark doubt that crept into the edge of her thoughts. "Really," she muttered out loud and climbed the stairs to her room. He had promised her to offer Applegate to her father first. Not that she needed to worry about that. She had a plan and she needed to stick with it. If she could get Alex to quit gambling, then he would be home more. If he were home more, she would see to it that she was always nearby.

Proximity would give him the chance to fall in love with her. She touched her lips and remembered the kisses they had shared. She thought about the book she had read the night before.

A little proximity might be exciting.

She shook her head at her wayward thoughts and locked the bedroom door. She went to the window and flung it wide open. A stark northern wind blew through, refreshing her muddled mind. She leaned against the sill with a tired sigh. Even if she lost the bet and he sold Applegate, she would continue her attempt to make him fall in love.

For she was convinced that when he fell in love with her she would be redeemed. Besides, she thought as she stifled a yawn, a man in love will do anything for his lady. Even buy back a stallion he once sold.


"What did she clean this time?" Alex asked Mrs. S. as he took another bite of pancake.

"She went through the library."

Alex swallowed hard. "All of it? What did she do with the contents?" He grabbed a cup of coffee and washed down his amazement.

"Well, most of it got pushed into the center of the room. There was no way she could have gone through all of it in a day. We did manage to get the foodstuffs properly stored and I believe she is concocting an elaborate scheme for storage and cataloging." She bustled over and cleared the table. "If you want my opinion, you really should do something with those things—especially all that silk . . . before it rots."

"What do you suggest I do with it?" he asked and watched her clear the table. She put the dishes in the sink, turned and looked at him, arms akimbo. "You're a bright man, Alex Laird. I think you can come up with an idea on your own."

"Did she tell you she wanted to sell it? Because I'm not selling it." He stood up.

"She didn't say a word," Mrs. S. said. "Shame on you for thinking that she did. Why don't you go take a look at the library and the den one more time? Take a long hard look at all that young lady has done. When you're done looking, I believe you'll think of the right thing to do."

Alex did as she suggested. He worked his way down the winding path that went through the dining room and into the hall. He touched boxes as he went. He liked all his boxes. They represented his worth. They represented his talent. How could she suggest that he get rid of them?

The door to the library stood open. He stepped inside in wonder. He'd forgotten how beautiful the wood trim in this room was. The uncovered sections of floor had been polished and the books dusted until their leather spines gleamed. He walked around the room, glancing at titles. He filled with pride. He'd forgotten how grand his library collection was. Why it put the Statehouse library to shame.

Alex sat down on a leather chair that Amelia had placed near the fireplace, put his feet on the footstool and pictured himself a cultured man, spending hours simply reading. He laughed. He never considered himself a gentleman and reading was something he rarely did anymore. Still, the room would look even better when the boxes were removed. Mrs. S. said that Amelia was thinking of the fourth floor for storage. If he remembered right, the nursery was on that floor. Come to think of it, that would be the best place to store things.

Amelia would soon be gone and he would never have any children to put there. Pushing out of his seat, he heard something crumple under him. Curious, he lifted the cushion to find Amelia's oversized apron stuffed underneath.

The crumpling sound came from the pocket. He reached inside expecting to find the latest inventory list. What he found made his mouth go dry. It was a list all right. A list on how to make a man fall in love. If that wasn't bad enough, he also found a book. A very interesting book.

He glanced through the pages and knew he was in a lot of trouble. While he was away, Amelia had been doing some plotting of her own. The introduction to the book claimed that if a woman knew what she was doing, she could get anything she wanted from a man.

Alex slammed the book shut. The little wench was trying to seduce him. A bead of guilt stirred in him. She'd almost succeeded . . . more than once. So, she wasn't as naive as he thought. He suddenly realized that what he thought was his private battle had become an all-out war. He would surely have to stiffen his resolve if he hoped to be finished with this affair once her father came.

He looked up. His first impulse was to confront her with the evidence, but he hesitated. Sometimes it was better to hold your cards close to your vest and this just might be one of those times. He put the list and the book back in the pocket and laid the apron on the chair.

Good thing she had gone to bed. It would give him time to prepare for whatever came next.

By 2 P.M. Amelia was up and dressed in a solid-colored day gown. She wrapped yet another big apron around her and she and Mrs. Strasburg moved her bed into the bedroom at the top of the stairs.

"This is a lot of work for a man who doesn't sleep," the older woman groused.

Amelia muscled the feather tick onto the wooden slats. "He said that this was the most comfortable bed in the house. It's only right that he should sleep in it."

"It would be better if you slept in it with him."

Amelia straightened. "Well, now, that's Alex's choice, isn't it?"

"You married him."

"Yes, and since it was a rather abrupt decision, I think it only fair to give the man some room to get comfortable with the idea."

"A man doesn't need room," Mrs. Strasburg said unfolding a fresh sheet. She gave Amelia an edge and they floated it over the bed. It smelled of lavender and sunshine. "It seems to me he is waiting for you."

"All he would have to do is ask." Amelia shook her head. "No, I think there's more to it than that. As best I can tell, Alex doesn't do anything without a reason. I've simply got to wait and see what his reason is."

"What kind of reason would keep a young man from sleeping with his new wife?" the older woman asked as they tucked the sheet around the mattress filed with down and fresh straw.

"Perhaps he's shy," Amelia suggested. "Or perhaps he's tender-hearted and needs to be wooed."

"Please," Mrs. S. said with a chuckle. "When it comes to pretty women, men never need to be wooed."

"Really . . . you think I'm pretty? I mean, I've been told I was passable . . ."

"I've seen the way he looks at you."

"How does he look at me?"

"Like a small boy looks at a candy store window. He looks as if he wants in, but he doesn't want to pay the price."

Amelia fluffed a pillow. "That's ridiculous."

"Is it?"

"Of course it is. Alex is the man of the house. I'm not asking him to pay for anything."

"Aren't you?"

What do you mean by that?"

"I mean, he knows you married him for that horse."

"So?"

"So maybe he wants more."

"Like what?"

"Maybe he wants love." The older woman fluffed a pillow with alarming strength. "Do you love him?"

"I don't know. I'd never thought of it like that. He's a good man. Maybe I could love him."

"If what?"

"I beg your pardon?"

The older woman stopped and put her hand on her hips. "You said that maybe you could love him and I heard a big if. As in maybe I could love him if what?"

Amelia sat down on the bed. "Don't you think it's terrible to see so much potential in a person going to waste? I mean, Alex has all of this." She waved her hand. "He simply stores it away. I've gotten to know him a little bit and I believe he could be so much more than a gambler. He could be a gentleman farmer. He could be a horse breeder. Why with Applegate he could easily found a dynasty. Our great grandchildren could be known for the quality of their horses." She glanced at Mrs. Strasburg. "Don't you think he's wasting his life?"

"Sounds to me like this dynasty you speak of is your dream, Amelia, not his. A man lives his life the way he sees fit. It's up to the woman to love him for who he is not who she thinks he should be."

"But Mr. Strasburg is so reliable. Why he practically takes care of this whole estate. It makes him so easy to love."

The older woman laughed. "Let me tell you something. When I met Bert, he was working for Mr. Engle, the former owner. His job was to shovel out the stalls and keep the stable clean."

"Oh."

"Hmm, yes, not a pretty job, and Bert had talent. He makes lovely wooden toys. He showed them to me once. They are so beautiful." She took a deep breath and let it out in a long sigh. "I think I fell in love with him the day he showed them to me. It was as if he were showing me his soul."

"But—"

"I saw his potential and began to calculate. I thought he was the man for me. I thought we would become famous toy makers and live in a grand house."

"What happened?"

"We got married and lived in a tiny crofter's hut behind the stable. I spent years pushing him to make toys. Why, once I even took some of his toys into town and sold them. I got quite a sum for them too."

"What did he say?"

"Bert was furious."

"Why?"

"His toys were *his*." She smoothed the cover. "I don't know how else to say it, but he felt that I had sold his children without his permission." She looked at Amelia. "You see, if he had gone into the toy business, he would have turned his soul into work. Yes, we would have had a big house, but Bert would have been miserable."

"I see, so what happened?"

"I had to do some serious soul searching of my own. I think I realized that I still loved him, even if all he ever amounted to was a stable boy. You see, if you love a man, then you accept him and his reasons for being who he is, even if they don't make sense to you."

"But other women mold their men into greatness."

"Trust me, they aren't happy and neither are their men."

"But what a waste . . ."

"Only God can make a person and he makes each of us only once. Then he lets go and watches what we choose to become." She nodded. "Now, I've got sheets for the smaller bed we moved into your room. I'll go get them. Why don't you think about what I've said." She left Amelia alone.

Amelia laid her head back on the bed. It was soft but crunched from the ticking. The smell of sweet hay and lavender rose around her. She tried to imagine loving someone enough to just let them be. She wasn't sure she knew how to do that.

She rolled over and surveyed the room. The bed looked good in here. It was a perfect fit. She got up and strolled over to the big oak armoire. Opening it, she saw his clothes were neatly folded inside and noticed that there would be enough room for her things as well.

She traced her fingers along the smooth edge of the cedar shelf and sighed. Love was far more complicated than she had thought. True love meant sacrifice. She wasn't sure she was up to the task.

Alex let out a long sigh. Whoever had been sneaking around his house had been at it for a while. Angry that he hadn't noticed it before, he counted the empty boxes stashed strategically throughout the house.

They'd been stealing from him systematically. He had so many things stored haphazardly that he would have never known about the stealing if Amelia hadn't said anything.

He picked up an empty box and tossed it aside. So much for collecting riches. He ran a hand though his hair. He had known these things could go away at any time, but he had thought he would lose them fairly.

Stealing was not fair. His blood boiled. He wanted to catch these people and when he did he would haul them down to the sheriff. Then he'd talk with the marshal and make sure they were sent to prison for a very long time. He shook his head. If it weren't for Amelia . . .

She had been right about carefully cataloguing his things and seeing to their proper storage. Funny he hadn't worried about this house or even the stuff inside before he had gotten married. His life had been about winning, not the spoils.

Now, perhaps it was about more. When Amelia left him, he wanted to give her enough to set her up in a fine house. He could see her serving tea in a nice dress and helping with some charity project.

A picture of how he imagined her in the future came to mind. The afternoon light would spill through a window as she looked up and smiled at him. His heart leaped in his chest. In his imagination her expression was filled with love and acceptance.

He shook off the image. It wasn't ever going to happen. Still the idea had pierced a small hole in the shield around his heart. He knew he'd have to patch that hole after she left. In the meantime, he would enjoy looking at her and when she lost the bet he would enjoy her unconditional love. Even if it were only for a few days.

Dinner time came and went. Amelia let out a deep sigh. She had to face facts. The man was a beast, but if she was going to love him, she would have to learn to love that beast.

She lifted the skirts of her evening dress and made her way to the kitchen. The smell of ham and sweet potatoes filled the air. Mrs. Strasburg had made applesauce, rolls and green beans. There was a fine fish soup for the first course and a nice fruit compote for the last.

"He didn't come in."

The cook stirred the soup, filling the air with onion and

leeks. She put the lid on the savory soup and turned to Amelia. "Did you tell him what time you had planned on eating?"

"Yes. I saw him with Mr. S. in the conservatory this afternoon."

"Well, they must have gotten busy and forgotten."

"Then I think I'll go remind them," Amelia declared and grabbed a jacket off the peg near the back door. "I won't have you go to all this trouble just to be ignored."

"Here, take this lantern." The older woman handed Amelia a tin lantern with a bright flame. "I believe that they have been building a trap for the robbers. The last thing you need to do is to accidentally spring it."

Amelia shrugged into the jacket and took the lantern. "I'll be careful." She opened the back door and stepped out into the crisp dark night. The air was so cold it took her breath away. She wrapped the jacket close around her and lifted the lantern.

She figured it was best to stick with the stone pathway that wrapped around the house. "Alex," she called. The stones were cold under her feet. She wore her best evening slippers and they were not made for warmth. The slippers were part of her campaign to win Alex's love. Step one, *Always take the time to look your best.*

"It doesn't help to look your best if the man doesn't come home to see it," she muttered to herself.

Rounding the corner, she found a small fenced garden that jutted out from the ballroom. In the dark the bushes looked like robbers hiding in the shadow. She swallowed her nervousness. "Alex, are you there?"

The gate to the garden was flanked by twin lion statues. Their eyes seemed to glow red from the lantern light, their expressions fierce. "Well, you should scare off robbers," she said and touched the lion's mane. Cold radiated up her fingers. She opened the gate and wandered toward the house. "Alex?"

"Amelia, what are you doing?"

She nearly dropped the lantern. Alex separated himself from the shadow of a particularly large bush. "Oh my, you frightened me."

"Good," he said grimly and took the lantern from her numbed fingers. "You should be frightened. It's not safe to be wandering around out here in the dark. Listen."

She did as he asked. There was the sound of silence that came with the first frost. A heavy silence that hung in the cold air. "What am I listening for?" she whispered.

He took her hand. "Come on, I'll show you."

A low rumbling sound grew in intensity as they moved toward the edge of the garden. "Now can you hear it?"

"Is that the lake?"

He raised the lantern and illuminated the edge of the garden. The land simply fell away. Underneath were the sounds of waves crashing against the rocks. "There is no fence on this side. You could have wandered right over the edge and fallen into the lake. We'd never have known what happened."

"I had no idea the cliff was so close."

He put his hand on the small of her back and turned her toward the house. "What were you doing outside anyway?"

"I was looking for you."

"Why?" His dark eyes glistened in the lantern light.

"You missed dinner," she said trying not to sound too accusing. "Mrs. Strasburg went to a lot of trouble to make something special."

"Why would she do that?"

"Because she knew you would be home."

"Hmm, must have skipped my mind."

"How can dinner skip your mind?" She grew impatient with him. "Aren't you hungry?"

He opened the garden gate and guided her past the stoic lions. "Sure, I could eat."

"Good, there's practically a feast inside waiting for you."

"Is this some female attempt to civilize me?"

"Whatever do you mean?" She was glad for the darkness for she could feel the blush that rushed up her cheeks.

"I mean dinner, the dress you're wearing under that jacket, those impractical shoes on your feet. It sounds as if you went to a lot of trouble."

"Well, I'm not asking you to dress for dinner. Simply eat."

He laughed. It came out a short bark. "Honey, I am dressed. In fact, this is probably the most dressed you'll ever see me." He held up the lantern and she saw that he wore a thick coat, a scarf, gloves, a work hat and thick work slacks. It looked at once manly and attractive.

"Well, at least you're practical," she said and ignored the reaction her heart had to just looking at him.

He held the door open for her and she brushed him as she stepped inside. For a moment his arms were around her. She could feel his warmth, smell his rich scent mixed with bay rum and the outdoors.

Surprised at this sensual reaction, she glanced up to see that he was only a breath away. His chin was darkened by a late afternoon shadow. His lips were full and inviting, and yet his gaze teased her. It was as if he dared her to resist him. She caught herself a second before she kissed him. "Mrs. Strasburg will serve dinner as soon as you are ready."

He crowded her through the door. The heat of the kitchen swept over her like a blanket. She took off the coat and hung it back on the peg. He took off his hat, gloves and coat and hung them beside hers. There was something oddly intimate about removing clothes beside this man. She swallowed hard and tried not to think about it too much. She stepped toward the dining room.

"The table's not set," he said walking over to the kitchen sink to wash up.

"We're eating in the dining room tonight," she replied. "We need to talk and I thought it was the perfect place to have a nice meal."

"Let me guess, you've stashed away all my things from yet another room."

"No need to worry," she said airily as she opened the adjoining door. "I have the inventory list in my pocket."

"That's not all you have in your pocket," he mumbled.

"I beg your pardon?" she asked, uncertain what he meant.

"Nothing . . . after you."

His cavalier answer perturbed her. How like him to say something and then not own up to it. She stepped into the dining room and took a deep breath. Really, sometimes Alex could be so ungrateful. Just like a beast.

## Chapter Ten

It was a scene set for seduction. The room had been cleared of most of the boxes. The wainscoting, polished with lemon oil, shone rich in the candlelight. A large mahogany table covered with a snow-white linen cloth sat in the center. A centerpiece of the bright oranges, reds and yellows of late fall flowers and leaves sat between two long tapered candles.

Gold chargers held china bowls set for the soup course. Enough polished silver for five courses lay alongside the chargers. Tall stemmed glasses, one filled with water and another half full of ruby-colored wine sat at the head of each place. The room smelled of fresh bread, savory ham and polished wood.

Hanging on the walls were paintings in rich burgundy and dark green depicting scenes of picnics and holiday meals. The colors matched the velvet curtains that covered the windows. Amelia waited for Alex beside the fireplace. She seemed to study the fire. He wondered what secrets she found there and if she would share them.

He was drawn to her. Her back was rigid, her head bowed. The gown she wore was a lovely color that mirrored her extraordinary eyes. She simply took his breath away. He found himself wondering what it would be like to come home to this every night.

He shook the thought away. He had to be strong because she would never be happy with a gambler. No, the man who would come home to her and win her heart would be more than a mere gambler. That man would give her those dreams of horses and children.

"I'm sorry that you had to come looking for me," he said and put his hand on her shoulder. The silk was soft and warm from her skin. It made him want to run his hand along the line of her shoulder to her neck, perhaps to cup her cheek and draw her sweet mouth toward him. Instead he stepped back.

She turned, her eyes unreadable behind her glasses.

"You've done a great job on this room. I have no idea how you accomplish so much in one day."

"I have help."

"You do?"

"Mrs. Strasburg and even Mr. Strasburg help me out." She reached into her pocket and withdrew a folded piece of paper. "I have the inventory of the things we took out of this room. I decided it was safest to store them in the nursery. It's on the fourth floor and there is a lock on the door."

He took the paper and stuffed it in his pocket along with his hands. "Thanks. Looks like you went to a lot of trouble." He glanced toward the table. "Shall we eat?"

"All right," she said. He took his hands out of his pockets and guided her by the small of her back. He couldn't help it. He took a deep breath as she walked beside him. Today she smelled of cookies. It made his mouth water.

He pulled out her chair and waited for her to sit. Her auburn hair was done up in a beautiful fall, and his hands itched to let it down. He wanted nothing more than to see her hair curl about her bare shoulders.

"Alex?"

He blinked. She looked at him as if he had lost his mind. In a way he had for he was torturing himself with thoughts of things that would never be.

"I've never sat at the head of a table," he said and took his seat. He picked up his napkin and placed it in his lap. "I see you didn't opt to sit at the other end."

"With it being just the two of us, I thought it would be uncomfortable," she said. "Don't you think?"

"Sure." He picked up his wine. It tasted of warm, sharp grapes. It burned softly as it flowed down his throat, relaxing him.

She reached up and put her hand on his. "I thought since the dining room is clear, we could start having dinner together every night."

Her hand was warm on his, and delicate by comparison. He turned his own over so that he covered hers. His thumb ran over the tiny bones along the back of her hand. Her skin was exquisite, like soft porcelain.

"Alex?"

He glanced at her. "Yes?"

"Is it all right if we have dinner together every night? I thought it would be a nice way to talk."

Talking was far from what his wayward emotions wanted, but she looked at him with such earnest that he gave in, even though he knew it was all part of her plan to seduce him. "Sure, that would be fine."

She smiled and sat back with a look of satisfaction on her face. She squeezed his hand and picked up her wine glass. "So, tell me what you did today. Mrs. Strasburg said she thought you and Bert were working on a trap for the burglars."

"Yes," he said and took another sip of the wine. He wondered if she knew that a drop of wine rested on her bottom lip. She must have felt it because she licked it away.

The movement went straight to his heart. Any sane man in his position would have run as fast and as far away as he could. Right now, Alex didn't want to be sane. The air was thick with things he hadn't felt in years. Things he wanted to savor no matter how fleeting.

Mrs. Strasburg came in and ladled soup into their bowls. She winked at Alex and went back into the kitchen. "Why do I feel as if there is a conspiracy going on here?" he asked as he dipped his spoon into the soup. It was hot and salty and the best he'd had in a long, long time.

"There's no conspiracy," she said. "I simply explained to Mrs. S. that you have been nothing but kind to me and I wanted to show my appreciation."

"Well, you've done that," he said and took another spoonful. "This is great."

"It's my sister Maddie's recipe."

He stopped his spoon halfway from the bowl. "Do you miss your family?"

She shrugged. "A little I suppose. Father and Beth were gone all summer. Maddie is newly married so I didn't get to see much of her, and my brothers . . . well they are brothers. You know how that is."

"No, I don't know," he said. "I'm an orphan."

"Truly?"

"Have you met any of my family?"

"Well, no, but I thought perhaps you'd had a falling out."

"Over my occupation?"

She had the grace to blush. He put down his spoon. "I was abandoned when I was very young. All I knew was my name and that my parents were dead."

"How horrible. What happened to them?"

"It's vague," he said and took a gulp of wine. "Something about a carriage accident or perhaps it was a fever." He shrugged. "Anyway, the rent was not being paid and the landlord packed me up and left me on the doorstep of the nearest orphanage. I took one look inside and decided I was better off on my own."

"So, you lived on the streets? How could you do that? Weren't you cold and hungry?"

"Human beings are more resourceful than you know. After a while I discovered I had a knack for cards. So I took up the profession."

"Didn't you go to school?"

"No."

"Then how do you know how to read and write?"

"I used to go to a library to warm up on really cold days. The librarian took pity on me. She brought me cocoa and taught me how to read and figure."

He thought about the woman who had been the closest thing to love he had ever known. She'd had dark hair and big brown eyes that she covered up with glasses. She would let him sit close enough to her that he could smell the rosewater she wore, and when she taught him something she always had a ready smile and a kind word of praise—a real luxury to the boy he had been.

"How very kind of her."

"Hmm." He took another swallow. "She asked me once to come and live with her. She promised we would be like family, but first I would have to give up gambling."

"How old were you?"

"Thirteen."

"What happened?"

He gave a short derisive laugh. "I tried to be what she wanted me to be, but it was too hard. Before I knew it I was back to gambling. One day I came home with my pockets stuffed with wads of cash from a particularly good pot. She demanded to know where I got the money. She thought I'd stolen it."

He took another sip of wine while Mrs. Strasburg cleared away the soup and brought out the next course. "I told her that I was not a thief, that I had won it fair and square."

"What happened? Did she believe you?"

"She notified the police. They took me off to be tried as a thief."

"No!"

"Yes," he said and pushed the green beans around on his plate. "I managed to slip away from the jail, but I lost all my winnings."

"What happened to the librarian?"

"I don't know. I never went back."

"Surely she must know what a terrible mistake she made."

"In my experience, people often see only what they want to see. When I didn't shape up to be the boy she wanted me to be, she washed her hands of me."

Amelia was silent for a long moment. Then she looked at him. "Is that what you think I will do? Do you think that if you don't become what I want you to be that I will leave you?"

His heart pounded at the possibility. He put on his best poker face to keep her from seeing his fear. Still his hand shook a little as he cut into the ham. He lifted one shoulder. "You will do whatever you need to do."

"What does that mean?"

He put down his fork and looked her square in the eye. "It means that you want a gentleman farmer or a horse breeder. I am neither of those things and the probability that I will become those things is very low."

"So, you're telling me that you won't even try those

things? Not even with all this to get you started?" She waved her hands around as if to point out what he had.

"I am now, and will always be, a gambler, Amelia. I cannot change."

"You mean you will not change." She stood up and tossed her napkin on the table. He stood up with her, emotions running high.

"You married a gambler, Amelia. That's what I'm telling you. All the pretty dresses and all the fancy dinners won't change that."

"No," she said, tears welling in her eyes. "Only you can change that." She shook her head. "I feel sorry for you. I'm sorry that you will never know all the wonderful things you can do, all the wonderful things you can be." She trembled with emotions he couldn't read. The pain of her words sealed the opening she had made in the armor around his heart.

"I am what I am," he replied. "No one can change that. Now it is up to you to choose to accept it . . . or not."

She studied him for a long moment. Her expression unreadable. "Good night, Alex."

"Good night."

She stormed out of the room, but her sweet scent lingered. He sat down and picked up his glass of wine. There it was. The truth had cut through both their dreams.

He dreamed that she would love him for himself and stay with him of her own choosing. She dreamed that he could be someone else. His stomach turned, for if he changed to keep her, he still wouldn't have her love. Only the man she dreamed of would win that love and no matter how much he wanted it, he would never be that man.

It was a lesson he knew well. He tossed down the rest of the wine and got up. Dreams were fragile things. Like eggs, once shattered they could never be put back exactly the same.

A loud clatter woke Amelia in the middle of the night, with banging and rattling. She gasped, sat up, and pressed the covers to her chest. A quick look around told her that she was alone in her room. Someone screamed outside her window.

She was out of bed and pulling on her robe when the door swung open. Fear raced through her at the sight of a man in her doorway. Heart pounding, she shrank back into the shadows between the wardrobe and the door.

"Amelia? Are you all right?"

Relief washed over her at the sound of Alex's voice. She stepped into the light from the hallway. "Yes. What is going on?"

A loud moan from outside slid under her cracked window. Alex strode to the window, looked out, then shut and locked it.

"Alex?"

"I don't want you to sleep with your windows open. It's not safe."

"I like fresh air when I sleep." A loud muffled wail punctuated her comment. "What is that?"

"It's a burglar," he said. "Stay here and for goodness sake, don't open your window."

He left, closing the door behind him. From the crack under her door, she could see the lantern light retreat with him as he moved down the hall. Another wail had the hair on the back of her neck standing on end. She clutched her robe to her neck and eyed the window.

She was tempted to jump back in bed and pull the covers over her head, but the sound of a door opening and closing made her move toward the window instead.

Outside the moon was half full in the sky. The bare branches of the trees waved in the cold wind. Something dark moved on the lawn just under her window. She pressed against the cold glass to get a better look.

There was a man lying on the ground. He moaned inconsolably. She watched as Alex came through the garden toward the man, lantern in hand. Alex said something, but the closed window muffled his words.

The man put up his hands and moaned. Alex stepped closer. It was then that Amelia saw a second shadow behind Alex. She gasped. The shadow was taller than Mr. Strasburg. That meant only one thing.

There was a second burglar and Alex was in danger.

Amelia was not one to stand around and wring her hands in times of trouble. She was a Morgan and her father had taught her better than that. She opened her wardrobe and pulled out a small derringer. Her hands shook as she opened the box that held the ammunition and took out two bullets.

Alex was in danger and it was up to her to help. She loaded the gun as she left her room, rushing down the hall.

It was dark, but she had become accustomed to the stacks of boxes. In fact, she figured she could walk down the hall blindfolded if she had to. It was better to navigate it in the dark, she thought. If she lit a lamp the burglars would know she was there.

She hurried down the dark stairs, her bare feet silent on smooth wood. Her bedroom window was above the conservatory and she assumed Alex had gone out the library door. But the other man was behind him, so if she went out the conservatory door she'd be behind them all.

She slipped through the hallway and into the conservatory. The piles of boxes that Alex kept were a blessing and a

curse in this situation. The burglars couldn't see her but neither could she see them.

She eased over toward one of the doors at the end of the
greenhouse. It was dark and her heartbeat pounded in her
ears. She crept through the shadows and cautiously looked
through the glass. Nothing moved. she took a deep breath
and opened the door. An icy wind blew through it, carrying
the sound of moans and shouting. She eased out the door, the
frosty ground biting into her feet. Ignoring the cold, she
slipped like a shadow through the garden, remembering at
the last moment to keep to the pathways.

She had no idea what kind of traps Alex had set. From the
sound of the trapped man, they were not something she
wanted to encounter.

The night air reverberated with a shout and the sounds of
a scuffle. The second man must have attacked Alex! She hurried around the corner to see two shadows grappling. The
lantern lay on the ground leaning sharply to one side but still
giving off faint light.

The trapped man moaned and hollered.

"Stop or I'll shoot!" she shouted and pointed her pistol at
the grappling men. Fear made the pounding in her ears so
loud that it deafened her. She held her gun as still as possible.

The two men paused for a moment and looked at her. "I
mean it. I will shoot and I'm a very good shot." They did not
move. "Good," she said with more bravado than she was
feeling. "Now put your hands up and step away from each
other." She trained her gun on the bigger of the shadows,
guessing correctly that the other man was bigger than Alex.

"Don't move, Amelia," Alex said, his tone something very
close to fear. "I'm coming over there."

It was then that she noticed the shape of the big man's
right hand. "Alex, be careful, he has a knife."

"I'm far enough away now," Alex said.

Even so, she kept her gun trained on the big shadow while Alex picked up the lantern. She could see blood running down the side of his head from a cut at his hairline. The shadows from the lantern distorted his face.

"You look awful." She took a step toward him, fear and compassion in her heart.

"Stop!" he shouted, holding his hands out in front of him. "Don't move."

Uncertainty was added to the emotions running inside her, but she stood still. "Okay."

Alex turned to the other man. "I would advise you not to move either. I have bear traps set in random places off the path."

Amelia swallowed. Bear traps were very mean-looking spiked hinges that could clamp onto a limb and bite to the bone. "Alex?"

"It's okay, Amelia," he said and cautiously picked his way to her. "I know where the traps are set." He took the gun out of her hands and trained it on the man he had been fighting. "If there are any more men out there, I'd advise you to show yourselves or you'll end up like your buddy here, writhing in pain."

"There ain't no one else," the second man said, his hands still in the air.

"For your sake, you'd better be right."

"I'm right. It's just Orville an' me."

"It hurts, it hurts," Orville moaned.

"It could be worse," Alex said. "Now, who are you and what do you think you're doing on my property?"

"We heard that you stored your winnin's out here. So we just came out to take a look around. See if the rumors were true."

"What rumors?"

"That you were the winnin'est man in four states."

"So, you came out here in the middle of the night to check out a rumor?"

"Yeah, we didn't mean nothing by it."

"Ow, please, it hurts."

"Shut up, Orville," the second guy said. "Really, mister, we was just wanting to know if you was worth what they say you was."

"Did you see what you wanted to see?"

"We seen that you have all this stuff just kind of layin' around." He shrugged. "Honest, mister."

"And you figured, since I had so much I wouldn't miss a little something."

"I swear I didn't take anything."

"Drop your knife and empty out your pockets."

"What?"

"I said drop your knife and empty out your pockets."

The man let the knife fall to the ground, then put his hands down and turned his jacket pockets inside out. Two silver candlesticks fell to the ground.

"Didn't take anything?"

"I brought those from home," the man said. "I swear. They're for my own protection."

"This is ridiculous," Amelia said and took a step forward to retrieve the candlesticks. Alex stopped her cold with a hand on her arm.

"I said stand still," he growled.

"Oh, right, bear traps," she said and swallowed. "It's just that those candlesticks look like the ones that were on the dinner table."

"Trouble, Mr. Laird?" Mr. Strasburg asked, breaking into the conversation as he came up the path with a rifle in one hand, lantern in the other.

"Help me," Orville said. "I'm hurt bad."

"Got one caught in our little trap, I see," the old man said and pointed his rifle at the other man. "What do you want me to do?"

"Let's get these two tied up and taken into town. I think the sheriff will be happy to open his jail cell for the night."

"But I'm hurt," Orville wailed. "I need a doctor."

"You need something all right," Mr. Strasburg said. "Now, you there with your pockets open, take four steps forward."

"Four steps?"

"Yeah, four steps unless you want to end up like your friend here."

Amelia watched as the man kept his hands in the air and took the four steps. Mr. Strasburg picked his way across the lawn until he came up behind the robber. Then he pulled the man's hands behind him and tied him up.

"Do you really have other bear traps?" Amelia whispered to Alex.

"Yes, I really do," Alex said, his dark gaze serious. "That's why I told you to stay in the house."

"I see," Amelia said. "Just how many traps do you have?"

"Enough." He waved the lantern and the light glinted off metal a few feet in front of her.

"Oh." She realized she had come fearfully close to stepping in one of the traps.

"Come on," he said and took hold of her hand. "I'll walk you safely inside."

"What about the robbers?"

"Mr. Strasburg can handle those two." He pulled her toward the path. The trip back to the conservatory door seemed a lot longer than she remembered.

"Is there a trap between here and where I found you?" she asked with morbid curiosity.

"One or two," he said with grim certainty.

Amelia swallowed the nausea that rose at the thought that

she might have stumbled into one. "You should have warned me."

"I did when I told you to stay in the house."

They arrived safely at the door. Amelia turned to Alex in the lantern light and gasped. His face was swollen. "You should come inside and let me take care of that."

"I have a few things to do before I can get cleaned up."

"I'm not going in if you aren't," she said, her stubborn streak kicking in. The wind whipped her hair out of its braid. Its long tendrils floated past her. The brisk wind lifted her night skirt and twisted it around her ankles. She had to stifle a shiver.

"Go inside, you're half frozen." He handed her the gun back, butt first. "Take this if you don't feel safe."

"It's not about my feeling safe," she said and took the gun. "I need to know that you are safe."

"I've been taking care of myself for a lot of years, Amelia. I'll be fine."

She reached into the pocket of her robe and pulled out a clean handkerchief. She dabbed at the blood that refused to quit trickling down the side of his face. "You don't look fine."

He took hold of her wrist. The heat of his skin sent a shiver along her arm. His gaze bore into her as if he was searching her soul.

"Having you out here won't keep me safe," he explained gently. "I know where the traps are and you don't. If you wandered into one, I would never forgive myself." He ran his hand along her wrist, easing her away from him. "Please go inside now. I'll be in after a while and you can play nurse then."

She studied his expression but found no give. It was clear they were both going to stand there until one of them gave in and from the set of his jaw it was going to have to be her. She let out a long sigh. "Fine."

"Good." The relief in his face hurt her feelings.

"Not because I can't take care of myself," she pointed out.

"Right." He took her by the shoulders and turned her toward the open door. "Go straight inside and lock the door behind you."

"If you don't come inside in the next thirty minutes, I am coming back out."

"I'll be in before then."

"Fine. I'll be waiting for you in the kitchen," she said.

Then he did the most amazing thing. He drew her against him and pressed a soft kiss to her temple. "Thank you," he said.

His body heat was a stark contrast to the cold wind and she wanted nothing more than to lean against him. To turn and feel his lips on hers one more time. The longing tore at her heart as she realized that she might have lost him to the robbers. It had been a very close call.

He pushed her gently away. "Go before you catch your death."

She went to the door and took hold of the knob. She glanced over her shoulder to see him watching her. "I'll be waiting," she said and stepped into the darkness inside. The door closed roughly behind her. The four windowpanes rattled with the wind as she threw the thick bolt shut. Then she looked out through the wavy glass.

She could make out the flicker of the lantern as Alex moved off. She rested her hot forehead against the cool glass and closed her eyes. His kiss clung to her skin and did something strange to her heart. She pushed away from the door and blinked.

She put her hand on her heart. Her rapid heartbeat had her

trembling so deeply that she needed to sit down. It hit her then. The truth of her heart. She was falling in love.

"Amelia?"

She turned at the sound of Mrs. Strasburg's voice and took a deep breath. What she needed was to regain her perspective on the situation. She wasn't the one who was supposed to fall in love. He was.

## Chapter Eleven

He'd almost lost her.

The thought struck him as he waved Bert on. The estate manager pulled off in a wagon headed for town and the sheriff. The two robbers were tied up like hogs on the way to slaughter. One had his leg bandaged where they had removed the trap that had cut through his skin and anchored him to a chain.

The cold wind blew down the collar of Alex's jacket. He glanced up. The brilliant stars in the clear November sky winked at him, mocking him. He'd won the battle but lost the war.

Alex pulled up his collar and turned toward the house. They'd been married over three weeks. In that short time something awful had happened. He'd fallen in love with Amelia.

Alex shook his head. She was the most stubborn, ornery, beautiful woman he'd ever met. When she stood toe to toe with him all he could think about was how interesting all that passion would be in the bedroom. He'd tried to close his heart, but she had somehow eased her way in. Heck, she'd stormed in like a general taking a hilltop.

He heaved a sigh. It fogged in the night air. No one had ever taken the time to care for him. No one had ever risked his life for him like she had tonight. The thought of it made him hurt.

It was the very reason he couldn't touch her. She deserved so much more. If he touched her, before her father came to collect her, she'd be stuck with him the rest of her life. It was clear to him she hadn't thought about that. Not according to that list she had in her pocket.

The way he felt right now, forever had its appeal. Why the thought of her married to someone else, sharing a bed with someone else, made him want to wrestle a bear. Heck, he'd tangle with something even ornerier, like a wolverine. Alex grimaced. Even so he doubted the wolverine would win. He was that agitated.

Honor was a touchy thing—the *only* thing he had that he could call his very own. If he gave in to his emotions, he'd get to keep her, but then he'd lose the only thing he'd ever had. For a brief moment he considered that it would be worth the price.

He grabbed the smooth metal of the door handle and prepared to open the door. Gritting his teeth, he pulled open the door and stepped into the warm, scented air of the kitchen.

She waited for him, just like she'd promised. Her hair had escaped its braid in a riot of tangles. It fell about her shoulders, forgotten. She wore her robe over her nightgown and wrapped over it was a large apron. He glanced at the pocket but it appeared empty.

Her lovely expression held concern and, if he read her correctly, uncertainty.

"Is everything all right now?"

"Bert's taking them into town," Alex said and shrugged off his coat.

"Did you find out exactly who they were and why were they stealing from you?"

"They were a couple of old soldiers wandering through town. A few months back they heard about my winning reputation. Someone bragged on how I had won the entire contents of a freighter. So they figured they'd come see if it was so."

"They took one look in your house and figured you wouldn't miss a few things," she concluded.

"Something like that." He turned to hang his coat on a peg. She gasped and he swung around quickly. "What?"

"Your back," she said, her hands clutching the chair, her knuckles white. "You're covered in blood. Come on. Sit down and let me see."

He glanced over his shoulder but couldn't see anything. He moved his shoulders gently and took a seat. "I don't think I'm hurt bad," he said, trying to ease her concern. "Truly."

"That man had a knife," she said, stepping behind him. "He might have stabbed you. We need to get your shirt off. Shall I cut it off?"

"I can pull it off." He tugged his shirt out of his pants and pulled it over his head in one smooth move. The motion didn't hurt until he put his arms back down. The sight of the large bloodstain on the back of it made his back ache.

She took the shirt from him and put it in a bucket of cold water. Then she examined his back. He could feel her behind him. The heat from her body mingled with the scent of mint on her warm breath as she bent closer.

He swallowed hard when her gentle fingers touched his skin. It took all of his self-control—and honor—not to turn around and tug her into his lap, Not to kiss her soft mouth and taste her sweet breath.

"Looks like just the edge of the knife got you," she said and stepped away. The distance between them seemed a sudden loss. "I'm going to clean it and get a better look."

She moved to the stove and picked up the teapot. She brought it to the table and poured the steaming water into a basin. The movement brought her to within inches of him. He reached up and brushed a long strand of silken hair away from her face, tucking it behind her ear.

He trailed his hand casually down her neck and along her shoulder. He felt her shiver and it was all he could do not to grab her. But he had to stop. She was not meant for him.

She paused at his touch. He had been casual and flirtatious, but there was nothing casual between them now. She straightened when he pulled his hand away.

"A little soap and water will help this," she said, her voice a tad too breathy, her actions tellingly stiff. She was aware of him. He could tell. It made things sweeter, and more difficult.

When she moved away to put the teapot back on the stove, he realized that he had been holding his breath. He let it out slowly then inhaled her scent as she drew near. His heart pounded in his chest. He felt like a schoolboy with his first crush.

Alex clenched his hands in his lap to keep from touching Amelia. It didn't make it any easier that she was his wife. He tried not to dwell on the sweetness of her kiss, the care in her heart, the softness of the curves that were well within reach.

"You look pale," she said, concern in her voice. "Is the cut on your head bothering you?"

"No," he answered honestly, but she didn't believe him. Frowning, she stepped in front of him. She took his face in her smooth hands and tilted his head so that she could clearly see the cut over his left eye.

All he could see was the clear blue of her eyes through her spectacles. The blue had specks of grey, each dark enough to hold a mystery. They were mysteries he wanted to spend a lifetime figuring out.

"Well, it's bothering me." She turned and dipped a clean rag in the hot water. Then she lifted his chin in her hand and washed the outer edges of his wound.

Her touch was firm, yet gentle. He could feel her breath against his cheek. The flannel of her robe brushed against his bare chest. She stood between his legs. It was the only way to get close enough to attend to his cuts and bruises. Again he clenched his hands on his thighs.

"There," she said. "Now that it's clean I can see it's not as deep as I had feared." She turned her gaze on him. "You scared the devil right out of me, you know."

"You shouldn't have been looking," he croaked out of a suddenly dry mouth.

"I'm going to give you a piece of advice that my father gave me when I first learned how to shoot."

"What's that?" he asked and watched as she wadded gauze then pulled out a long strip of linen for a bandage.

She pressed the gauze to his wound and wrapped his head in the linen. Her arms went round and round him and he forgot to breathe.

He closed his eyes and imagined her arms around him for real. They would wrap around him and share his hurts and his joys.

"Are you listening to me?" she asked. He opened his eyes to see that she had taken a step back and now had her hands on her hips, scissors in one hand and the remaining linen in the other.

"Sorry," he said, his voice rough. "Headache. You understand."

"Oh," she said and scurried to the cupboard. "Of course.

Mrs. Strasburg keeps the headache powders in here." She opened the cupboard, moved a few things around until she found what she wanted. He took the moment to collect himself and regain his poker face.

She turned back with a look of concern. "You're flushed."

"Must be from the blood loss," he said with a straight face.

"I'll get you some water to take this with." She brought him a ceramic mug and handed him a dose of the bitter powder that promised to cure what ailed him. Alex took it, suffering the taste but washing it down with pure sweet water.

The water cooled his mouth but did little to cool his desire. "Thank you," he said and handed her the cup. "I'm sorry about before. What were you saying?"

She put the cup on the table and leaned against it so that she could look him in the eye. "I was giving you the same advice my father gave me when I first learned to hunt."

"You hunt?"

"No distractions," she chided. "Just listen. This is good advice."

"All right, please proceed."

"My father told me always to be aware of my surroundings. 'Amelia,' he said, 'as long as you keep in mind that wolves run in packs you'll survive.' "

"I see."

"Do you?"

"You're telling me that I should have expected there to be more than one burglar."

Her expression brightened so much he felt as if he'd won a blue ribbon at the fair. "Exactly. That's why I went to the window."

"You were watching out for me."

"Someone had to," she said and stepped around him. He

felt her soft touch on his back and realized that his shoulder throbbed.

"I've done a pretty good job watching out for myself for thirty years," he said, wincing when she probed a bit too hard. "What makes you think I need your help now?"

"Oh, I don't think you need me," she said a touch too lightly. "I know I need you."

Shock ran through him at her words and he turned to see her face. She was all business as she cleaned his wound. "You need me?"

"Yes, silly," she said and pushed him back to face the table. "You're my husband and the last thing I want is to be a widow. I don't know the first thing about running this estate."

"Oh." He felt foolish. She needed him but not in the way he wanted her to need him. "I'm sure the Strasburgs would give you good advice. Your father wouldn't let you do anything foolish."

"Well, I wouldn't want to do anything that might jeopardize Applegate."

He winced when she laid the steaming hot cloth on his wound. "So you weren't really watching out for me. You were watching out for that horse."

"Hmm," she said and wiped his back dry. "I suppose some people might think of it like that."

He blew out a breath and bit back the pain of her words. "Well, I thank you," he said as simply as possible. "I'm certain Applegate thanks you too."

"No need for thanks," she said as she tied a bandage around his shoulder. "As long as you have Applegate, you have me."

"Unless you lose all your toothpicks in our card game," he said as casually as he could. "Then I'll have you even after I sell the horse."

She leaned in so close her breath tickled the inside of his

ear. "What will you do when I win all of your toothpicks? Hmm?"

He reached up and grabbed her delicate wrist, tugging her into his lap. It was where he had wanted her all night. As stupid as it was, it felt so right.

"If you were to beat me at cards I would give you whatever you want, Amelia."

"Good," she said and brushed the hair away from his face. "Good."

"But I can't be something I'm not," he warned and ran his hands along her arms, taking in the feel of warm flannel and silky skin. "A bet, like a wish, can't change a human being."

"I know," she said with a quiet smile. "But it can give you a reason to try."

He sighed deeply. The woman was soft and sweet in his arms, yet still as stubborn as a mule. There was only one thing left to do. Kiss her.

Amelia felt the emotion in his kiss clear down to her toes. The kiss held a promise that brought butterflies to her stomach. She pressed herself against Alex in an attempt to absorb as much of the heat, emotion and pleasure as she could.

She ran her palms over his bare shoulders. He felt warm, but also like steel. The strength in his chest gave her a thrill she had not known before. His manly outdoor scent filled her. Just a hint of the iodine she'd used on his wounds kept her from getting too lost in the sensation. He had risked his life tonight and she had cared for him. Her heart fluttered.

There was hope for them both.

He drew her closer, wrapping her in the safe shelter of his arms. Perhaps he had finally fallen in love with her. Perhaps now they would have the marriage night she had read of in that book. Surely only love would motivate that kind of intimacy.

She settled her lips on his, drawing him in, tasting him, seeking the truth. Did he love her? Perhaps if she told him she loved him, he would understand that it was safe to love her in return.

"Alex," she said, her voice breathy.

"Amelia," he answered and kissed her cheek. He made her shudder with pleasure when he kissed her jaw and then trailed a group of kisses along her neck.

"There is something I think you ought to know," she whispered.

He continued kissing her, concentrating on the vulnerable spot behind her ear. She giggled at the rush of tingling desire that raced through her. "Alex, did you hear me?"

He made a sound in the back of his throat. She decided that he wasn't listening and what she wanted to say was too important to be ignored. She reached up and put her hands on either side of his face, forcing his attention. "Alex," she said as solemnly as she could, looking deep into his smoky eyes. "I want to tell you that I lo—"

Someone banged on the kitchen door, startling them both. Alex leaped up, careful to steady her on her feet before he tucked her behind him.

"Who the—"

"Open up!" came the demand from outside. The pounding of the door echoed the pounding in her heart. Amelia swallowed hard. It sounded like her father was at their door.

"Stay here," Alex ordered. He picked up a carving knife out of the drawer and moved to the door.

"I said open up this door!" came the demand. The pounding grew more intense.

"Identify yourself," Alex shouted as he stood in front of the door.

"Robert Morgan," came the reply. "I demand that you open this door and let me see my daughter."

"Papa?" Amelia took a step toward the door.

Alex held out his hand to stop her. "Wait," he said and leaned against the door. "Tell me your daughter's name."

"Amelia Morgan, now let me in."

Alex glanced her way. Amelia wrapped her arms around herself. It was her father and she had never heard him sound this angry in her life. "Open the door, Alex."

He opened the door carefully. Her father pushed his way through like a bull in a rage. The cold wind blew in, making the lanterns flicker and the fire leap all over the fireplace. "Amelia?" Papa's dark blue eyes took in far too much before they settled on her. "So, it's true."

"Papa!" Amelia threw herself into her father's arms. She gave him a big hug and a kiss on the cheek. "What are you doing here?"

Henry slid into the room and closed the door behind him, cutting off the icy wind. A few frozen leaves scattered across the kitchen floor. "I've been looking for you," her father said in a gruff voice.

"Well, you've found her," Alex replied.

Amelia glanced at him. He didn't look very happy. Her brother Henry came in wrapped in a giant duster, his hat pulled over his eyes, his shoulders slumped.

"Henry!" Amelia ran to her brother and gave him a hug. She missed her family. Up until this moment she hadn't realized how much. "Come on in, both of you. Take off your coats. You've come a long way. You must be hungry. I have some leftovers I can warm. How about some coffee?" She realized that she was babbling, but as much as she was delighted to see them, the tension in the room was so thick she could cut it with the knife Alex still clenched.

"Alex," she said and touched his bare arm. "This is my father, Robert Morgan, and you remember my brother, Henry."

"I remember," Alex said not even looking at Henry. His gaze was locked with her father's in a tense battle of wills.

"Papa," Amelia said. "Papa, this is Alex Laird, my husband."

Her father looked at her. She knew that look. He reserved it for the worst of miscreants. She swallowed hard. "Well, now that we all know each other, I think I'll make some coffee."

No one moved. Her father and Alex returned to their silent battle and she sighed. She stepped purposefully between them. "Papa, let me have your coat." She reached up to help him out of it.

"We're not staying."

"Of course you are. You've come all this way and it is the middle of the night."

Her father grabbed her wrist when she tried to unwind his scarf. "I said we're not staying." His look bore through her. "We came to take you home where you belong."

"I belong here now, Papa. This is my home," she said as patiently as she could. "Alex is my husband. We've been married for weeks now." She turned to her brother. "Henry, you did tell Papa that we got married, didn't you?"

Henry answered with a shrug and seemed to shrink even further into his coat.

She frowned. "Well, we are married. I wore Maddie's dress. Ask Mrs. Selis. Better still, ask Sheriff Pickens. It was his idea."

"What was his idea? That you wear Maddie's dress or that you get married without a license to a man you don't even know."

"We had a license," Alex said.

Amelia was happy to hear someone on her side in this conversation. "Thank you," she said and turned back to her father. "We had a license. Henry went to the courthouse and brought us a special license."

Her father crossed his arms over his chest. "Tell me why you needed a special license?" His glare grew. "What, exactly, was the reason you had to get married so quickly?" He took a step toward Alex.

Amelia put herself between them. "He didn't do anything to me, Papa. In fact he has never been anything but a perfect gentleman."

Her father looked from her robed figure to Alex's bare chest and back. "Tell me another fairy tale."

"Papa!" Amelia said, aghast. She clutched her robe around her neck. For the first time in her life she was ashamed. Not for herself, but for her father. "We are married," she said again and this time took a step back toward Alex. "It's the middle of the night."

"She's not an heiress," Papa said over the top of her. "That horse is the only thing of value and it happens to have been mine."

"I beg to differ with you, sir. It was mine." Alex crossed his arms over his chest. "I won it in a card game."

"Yes, Henry told me," Papa said. "I'm disgusted with my son for betting something he didn't own, but marrying Amelia was not the answer."

"All I ever wanted was the horse," Alex said, his tone sincere but stubborn.

His words stabbed Amelia's heart. She had failed to make him fall in love with her after all. She had failed. "Alex?"

He looked her in the eye. "All I ever wanted was what was rightfully mine."

"Applegate," Amelia whispered and clutched her robe closer. Her heart was in her throat.

"I never touched her, sir," Alex told her father. He moved

away from Amelia toward the sink. "She wouldn't listen to reason that's why I went to the sheriff."

"But—"

"But Amelia would not let go of the horse," Alex said over the top of her protest. "So the good sheriff explained to your daughter that the horse belonged to me."

"She did insist on going with him, Papa," Henry piped up. "She insisted in front of the sheriff, so Sheriff Pickens said she'd have to be married before he'd let her go with him."

"So you married her," Papa said.

"I wanted what was rightfully mine," Alex said. "Now you've come to collect what is rightfully yours."

Amelia turned to Alex, uncertainty stuck in her throat. She suddenly felt sick. "Alex?"

"I knew you would come for her," Alex said, ignoring Amelia. It was as if she were already gone. She could barely breathe. "So, I never touched her," Alex went on. "I figured if you were a good father, you would come for her. An annulment is an easy enough thing to get."

"I don't want an annulment," Amelia said. She turned to her father, hoping he would stop this madness. "Papa, I'm married to Alex and I intend to stay married."

"There are ways of proving her purity," her father said.

"Papa!" Amelia could not believe they were talking like this. She glanced at Henry. Her brother shrunk farther into his coat, his eyes firmly on the floor.

"Do whatever you think you need to do," Alex said. "I'm a gambler, not a liar."

"I suppose you expect some sort of payment," Papa said as he dug his money clip out of his pocket.

Horrified, Amelia stepped toward him. "Papa, don't."

"Go get your things, Amelia."

"I will not."

"Put away your money," Alex said. "All I want is what is rightfully mine."

"I'm your wife," Amelia said. The horror of the moment made her numb inside. "That makes me rightfully yours."

"I never made you any promises, Amelia," Alex said.

"Without my permission, you were never rightfully his," Papa said. "Now, go get your things."

"But I thought—"

"You'd better go," Alex said, his eyes suddenly dull and cold.

Amelia glanced from Alex to her father. They seemed to have reached an understanding—a gentlemen's agreement in which she had no say. "I'm not a piece of property to pass around," she insisted, her temper boiling over. "I'm a grown woman and I can make my own decisions."

"Really?" Papa said, his bushy gray eyebrows lifting. "Do you want to stay and live with this man knowing that he married you only because you forced his hand?"

"I did not force him." She glanced at Alex. He looked surprised at her words and a pang of guilt flashed through her. "He could have said no at any time."

"And have you ruin your reputation by following him?"

"She threatened to live in his barn, Pa," Henry said.

Amelia sent her brother a look that made him step toward the door. "I never cared a fig about my reputation."

"That much is clear," Pa said, stuffing his money back in his pocket. He tugged on his gloves. "In a few months this will all be forgotten. Now, go collect your things. We've bothered this poor man long enough."

"But—"

"No more buts, Amelia. Go. With any luck we can be home by sunrise."

"Alex—"

"Get your things, Amelia," Alex said. He refused to look

at her, to help her. He wasn't going to fight for her. Suddenly it became clear to her that he was happy to see her go.

"Fine." She turned on her heel and stormed out of the kitchen. Tears welled in her eyes, but she refused to let them out. She'd failed in her attempt to make Alex love her. Instead she had fallen in love with him. Alex Laird was a gambler who vowed never to change his ways and still she loved him.

She quickly made her way through the familiar dark halls and up to her room. Once inside she closed and locked the door. She wanted to stay. The truth was that she wanted to spend the rest of her life with this stubborn man who refused to change.

Somehow over the last few weeks things had changed. She had changed. Her life was no longer about where Applegate belonged. Instead it had become about where she belonged.

## Chapter Twelve

He couldn't bring himself to watch her leave so he'd excused himself and gone to the stables. The horses welcomed him with curiosity in their gentle eyes.

"Hey, boy," he said when Applegate poked his head out to see what all the commotion was all about. The stallion nodded a greeting. His wide nostrils sniffed out the apple Alex had stuck in his coat pocket on the way out the door.

Alex pulled out the apple and fed it to the animal. "Well, she's gone, old boy." Alex stroked the animal's mane. "We both knew it was inevitable. It's just that I never expected it to hurt this much."

He sighed with a groan and gave the animal a last pat, then hunched into his jacket. "Okay, ladies, show's over. It's late, let's go to bed." He picked up his lantern and made his way to the tack room.

The room seemed smaller now. The cot was squeezed into the corner where he had left it. The chill wind swept in under the stable door. It rattled the tack room door and howled down the hall. Alex sat on the cot. The wool blanket felt rough against his hands. The scent of liniment and animals filled his nostrils and yet he could still smell Amelia's sweet candy scent.

Above the sound of the mournful wind came the sound of a carriage rattling away. Alex swallowed the loneliness that engulfed him. He grabbed the extra horse blanket and pulled it over his shoulder as he sank into the cot. Closing his eyes, Alex imagined Amelia in the carriage.

Would she be relieved? No, somehow he saw her as angry and he grinned in the darkness. Yes, she would be angry because the rescue wasn't her idea. Or better yet, she would be livid because her father had agreed that Applegate belonged to Alex. He thought about how she looked when she was angry. Her eyes flashed and she visibly trembled. It gave a man ideas about the kind of passion deep within her—passion that he had been fortunate enough to sample. Alex refused to feel guilty about the kisses he'd stolen. It was a small price to pay for the greater gift he had given her . . . her freedom.

One day, she would thank him for what he had done for her. Perhaps she would forgive him. He tugged the blanket around him and let out a long cloud of breath. Perhaps she'd even name her firstborn son after him.

Amelia wanted to kill them, do away with them all. *Men. Why on earth did God invent such hard-headed, simple-minded, unreasonable creatures?*

She crossed her arms over her chest and stared out the carriage window into the night. She refused to speak to either of the cursed males who rode with her in the carriage. She wished she'd had the chance to speak to Alex one more time, just to snub him.

Goodness, they were all idiots. How they decided that they knew best was beyond her. She glared at her brother out of the corner of her eye. This was all *his* fault. If the little weasel hadn't bet her baby, none of this would ever have happened.

She looked back out the window. If he hadn't lost that bet, she would never have met Alex. She would not have married in such a rush and she would not be making this mad dash in the middle of the night.

It was as if her father couldn't get her away fast enough. She flashed him an angry look, then turned her shoulder to him. How *could* he? How could he barge in and make accusations? How could he walk into *her* house and treat her like she was a two-year-old who had gotten lost and was staying at the neighbor's?

She was twenty years old for goodness sake and had a lot more sense than her brother Henry. Yet Papa had taken Henry's word over hers as if *she* were the fool.

It hit her hard, and it hurt. Maybe she had been a fool. Alex had told her father in plain words that he didn't want her. He had never wanted her.

Was the man stupid? How could he not want her? She was bright and helpful. He'd said so himself. She was a good companion and not all that homely to look at.

*"All I ever wanted was the horse."* Alex's words burned her. He had never loved her. He obviously believed he would never love her or he would have fought for her.

His kisses had meant nothing. The adventures they had shared were mere diversions to him. Shame engulfed her. She had tried and tried but failed to seduce him.

Yet he had never told her anything but the truth from the start. All he wanted was the horse.

Darn it, this was all *her* fault. How could she ever look him in the eye again? For that matter how could she look at her father? He had done his fatherly duty and rescued her from her folly.

How could she, plain old Amelia, have dared to dream?

She had tried desperately to bend reality to fit her dream, but it simply wasn't possible.

Alex thought fairy tales were grim, she remembered. Amelia now found real life even grimmer. It was going to be a very long, very dark ride home.

The following day was the longest of Alex's life. He spent the morning with the sheriff going over the burglary and how he'd caught the men. Then he'd spent time at the diner brooding over a good cup of coffee.

"What's the matter, honey," the waitress said. "I've never seen you this blue. Trouble with a card game?"

"No."

She cocked her head and contemplated him. "Woman troubles."

"What makes you say that?"

"You have the look of a man who has just lost his gal. What's the matter? She run out on you?"

"Something like that."

"Don't tell me she left you for another man."

"Don't be ridiculous."

"Well, then it was probably some kind of simple misunderstanding. You men do tend to have trouble with communication. What you need to do is, you need to go after her," she said. "Let her see how you feel."

"She'd never understand."

"Then you sit on top of her until she does understand, and if that doesn't work, why honey, take her to bed. I swear from the looks of you that ought to smooth things over just fine."

"I'm not going after her," Alex said and picked up his cup. "It's better this way."

"Oh, so it's better for you to mope around like your heart just got cut out."

"Yes," he said and nodded. "It's better."

"Men," the waitress muttered. "The whole lot of you don't think right."

Alex wished it were that simple but he knew in his heart it wasn't. He finished his coffee, put a quarter on the table, tugged on his hat and headed home. He passed the saloon and the regular card game but he knew better than to play today. He'd be an easy read.

Going home wasn't really a better option. There was too much of Amelia in the house. Heck, even his stable was off limits. Every time he looked at Applegate, he thought of Amelia.

He mounted his horse and headed out to the countryside, but the distractions didn't work. So he thought he'd ride into Milwaukee for a change of scene.

A week later he finally ventured back into the house. It was cold, the kitchen abandoned. He had told Mrs. Strasburg not to bother cooking anymore. He wouldn't be eating at home.

He shoved his hands into his pockets and walked through each room. Amelia had put a pretty large dent in the work that needed to be done.

For the first time in years, he looked at what he owned. Really looked at it, and realized that it was wasteful to let it sit piled in stacks of boxes. No wonder the robbers had wandered in. Those two-bit thieves had taken one look at his stash and realized that he didn't care enough to notice if it was all there.

They had confessed to collecting two wagons' full and he hadn't even missed it. That was just plain foolishness on his part. He went into his study and helped himself to a drink.

He leaned against the massive oak desk and remembered

the first time Amelia had chased him in here. How she had been determined that he not drink. How she had climbed the mountain of boxes until their heads grazed the ceiling.

He had teased her until she was so angry she hadn't even realized she'd shown him a good bit of leg as she scrambled up. His mouth was dry at the thought. His heart grieved from missing her.

Alex downed his drink in a single gulp and made a decision. He would bring in an appraiser and sell off the good stuff to his merchant friends. And he would auction off the rest. Better to have the cash in his pocket.

The quicker he could lose it all in card games, the better. He'd been losing all week. It would be easy to prove he'd been right to let her go. She didn't deserve to be destitute, and a gambler's wife could count on being destitute at least once in her life, if not more.

Alex didn't mind being destitute, but he refused to let it happen to someone he loved.

"Papa sent me up to talk to you," Maddie, Amelia's sister, said as she opened the bedroom door. "He said you've been up here for nearly two weeks straight and you haven't spoken to him since he brought you home. He is worried that you're wasting away."

Amelia turned her back on her sister. "I'm fine. Really."

"Right," Maddie said and pulled the curtains away from the windows. A thin ray of winter light shone in. It was cool and seemed to fit Amelia's mood. "You can't hide in here forever, you know."

"Why not?" Amelia snapped. She turned to her sister suddenly contrite. "I'm embarrassed, and angry with Papa for making such a point about my foolishness." She stood up and went to the window. "If I leave this room, I might say or do something I would regret later." She clasped her hands behind her back. "What I need is time alone to think."

"To think about what?"

"I'm afraid my whole life has been a fraud."

"In what way?"

"All I ever dreamed of was meeting the perfect man. He would be tall and handsome, smart and hard-working, and he'd take one look at me and fall in love." She wrapped her arms around her waist. "Together we'd breed the most magnificent horses and have many happy children."

"Just because you lost Applegate doesn't mean you can't have your dream," Maddie said gently. "Papa has several good breeders to give you for your dowry."

"Yes, yes, I know."

"Then what is it? Are you afraid no one will want you now because of your reputation? Because if that's what you think, I'm here to tell you otherwise."

"It's not my reputation. It has never been my reputation, though I am a bit nervous about the Ladies' Brigade."

"If not your reputation, then what?"

Amelia sat down on the bed. "May I ask you a personal question?"

"Sure."

"What did you do to get Trevor to fall in love with you?"

"What?"

"Was there something you did to make Trevor fall in love with you? Something anyone could do?"

"I certainly hope not."

Amelia looked down at the bedspread. "I was afraid of that." She smoothed the fabric, letting her fingers run over the three separate colors of blue. Amelia's room was decorated in blue to match her eyes. Her mother had done it when Amelia was very small and she had kept the color through the years. It gave her the feeling that her mother was near.

"I think I'm in love with him," she said in a weak voice. Tears welled in her eyes and she tried to blink back her emotion. "But I couldn't make him love me back."

"Oh, Amelia." Maddie pulled her into a warm cinnamon-scented embrace. "So, it isn't just about losing Applegate."

"No," Amelia replied and sniffed back the tears that threatened to break free. "I miss Alex." She pulled away from her sister. "I know it's ridiculous." She looked away. "He's nothing like I imagined my love would be. He's not a gentleman, not a farmer, not even a horse breeder. He's a gambler and that is all he ever wants to be. He kept telling me that, but I wouldn't listen. I thought that he had so much potential, that if only he would try he could be the man of my dreams and we could raise horses together."

"Oh, Amelia, you can't make a man be anything other than what he is," Maddie said. She reached up and tucked a strand of hair behind her sister's ear.

"I think I've figured that out."

"There will be other men, dearest."

Amelia stood up. "That is the crux of the problem. You see, I think I love Alex more than I love that old dream of mine. I know I love him more than I love Applegate and that's saying something."

"But you don't think he loves you."

"He told Papa he never wanted me, but he never actually said he didn't love me."

"Did you ever tell him you loved him?"

"No. I never showed him either. I was too busy trying to make things the way I thought they should be. I was always trying to change him. Why, I even went so far as to rearrange his house to fit my idea of a comfortable home."

"Oh, dear."

"I know," she said with a self-deprecating laugh. "Here I thought I was helping, but what I was doing was telling him that I didn't like who he was or how he lived." She took a deep breath and let it out slowly. "No wonder he didn't tell me he loved me. He must have thought I couldn't wait to be rid of him."

"Love is a very difficult thing," Maddie said. "It's easy to get caught up in your own expectations."

"I had no idea, and now I will never know. Oh, Maddie, I will never know if we really were meant for each other. I will never know if my heart was right, but my expectations wrong."

"You could still know."

"How?"

"You need to ask yourself if you love him for who he truly is. Can you love him unconditionally even if he is a gambler? What if he doesn't want children? What if he wants to move to California and take up gold mining? Is he still the right man for you?"

"A few months ago I would have said no. Applegate and my dream were too important to me."

"What changed?"

"I guess I changed. I've come to realize that life is not so easily planned out. That love can be a dream on its own."

"So what are you going to do?"

"Papa wants me to get an annulment."

"What do you want?"

"I want to see Alex one more time," she said softly. Not to snub him as she had first thought, but to give up the pretense and bare her heart. "I want to tell him that I love him unconditionally and that no matter what he decides to do with the rest of his life I will always love him."

She sat down. "I will leave it up to him to get the annulment. It is clear to me that even my loving him cannot make him love me in return."

"No, dearest, it can't."

"But I have to give it a shot."

"Then go do it. Get dressed in your finest dress and find your husband and tell him what you just told me. If he is fool enough to let you go, than he isn't worthy of your love."

"Yes," Amelia said feeling for the first time in weeks as if she had a purpose. "Yes. If I don't tell him, then I will never know for sure if my love would have made a difference."

"Come on then," Maddie said. "I'll go with you and we'll see what kind of man this gambler really is."

After two weeks back in his old ways, instead of feeling better, Alex felt worse, as if he had pushed everything good and right out of his life. He hated himself for letting Amelia go, and for being unbending about his profession. Darn it, he chose to be a gambler because he knew he was good at it. He refused to admit that the idea of being something else scared the devil out of him.

He hurt. It was clear to those around him that he was like a lion with a thorn in his paw. They circled wide and left him alone.

Alex was sitting in the darkest corner of the meanest saloon playing cards with the nastiest gamblers he'd ever come across. It was like the place where he had first learned to play—the place he recalled whenever he needed to remember who he really was. This was not a pretty card game. There was no finesse, no skill, only raw luck.

He swallowed a shot of rotgut whiskey to cover the stifling odor of unwashed bodies. Just being there made him feel low and mean. It fit his mood.

He reached down and fingered the latch on his gun belt. He prided himself on being a decent shot. He'd had to be to survive in places like this.

"What 'chu got, boy?" the grizzly man across the table asked.

"Aces over jacks," Alex said and slowly set down the cards. He kept his hand on the butt of his pistol. This was his fifth winning hand in a row. The natives were getting restless.

"Shoot," the thin man with the cigar said, and threw down his cards. "That's suspiciously lucky if you ask me."

"Nobody's asking you," the sweaty fat man on the left said. "But, heck, it sure beats my pair of threes." He laid his cards to the table.

Everyone looked at the grizzly old man. "I ain't never seen anyone so lucky at cards," the old man grumbled and threw down a pair of sixes and a pair of eights.

Alex reached out and dragged the pot toward him. "Lucky at cards, unlucky at love."

"What's matter, boy? Gotcha an itch ya cain't scratch?"

"Probably one of them ladies who don't like gambling," the thin man said and chewed on his cigar. "My ma was like that. 'Give up the cards,' she'd say. 'Or don't even think about coming home.'"

"Sounds like a woman," the sweaty man said as he grabbed the cards and shuffled them. "Once they got their hooks in a man, they never let him alone."

Alex shook his head. What these men didn't know was that he was in love with a lady too good for the likes of a gambler. When you reel in a prize fish, you can do only one of two things. Stuff it and mount it in your living room where it will look down on you for the rest of your days, or let it off the hook for someone else to catch and enjoy.

He'd let his prize go, and although it hurt like heck, he knew it had been the right thing to do.

"Excuse me gentlemen, do you have room for one more player?"

Alex nearly gagged at the sound of Amelia's voice. His

first reaction was denial, but the slack-jawed looks of the other men at the table left no room for doubt.

He turned around slowly to give her time to come to her senses and leave. "Amelia?" She stood there dressed in a smart little suit that showed off her figure and the color of her eyes.

"Hello, Alex," she said and smiled at him. He couldn't explain it, but that smile warmed him to his bones. It did more for him than any amount of rotgut whiskey could.

"What are you doing here?" he asked and stood up. This was not the place for a woman of breeding. Definitely not a place he ever wanted to see his wife—and she was still his wife.

"I came to play cards," she said. "May I?" She touched the empty seat next to him.

"No!" He couldn't help it. He saw the way these men looked at her. Like a pack of wolves catching wind of particularly juicy prey. He took her by the elbow and pulled her toward the door. "Does your father know where you are?"

"I don't answer to my father anymore," she said. "I'm a married woman."

He pushed her through the swinging door to find another young woman dressed in deep green pacing just outside. She rushed toward them. "Unhand my sister!"

"She may be your sister, but she is still my wife and I will put my hand on her if it will keep her out of a place like that."

"Alex, this is my older sister, Madeline Morgan, I mean, Madeline Montgomery. She just got married a few months ago. Maddie, this is my husband, Alex Laird."

He ignored Amelia's introduction. He couldn't get over her showing up in a saloon like that. It made him madder than a wet tomcat. "Do you two make it a habit of going into saloons?"

"Oh, no," Maddie said. "Amelia is the least likely to do anything so outrageous."

Alex raised an eyebrow at Maddie and looked at her knowing he had caught her in a direct lie. Her smile faded.

"Well, I'm sure you two have things to talk about. I'll be just across the street in the mercantile . . . looking for, um, ribbon." She turned on her heel and scooted across the street before Alex could think to stop her.

"How dare you?" Amelia said and pulled her elbow out of his grasp. Her eyes flashed beneath her glasses and she trembled with anger the way he remembered. "That was very rude."

He crossed his arms over his chest, satisfied to see emotion in her expression. "I never claimed to be polite."

She opened her mouth as if to say something, then snapped it closed. Instead she tugged on the edges of her crocheted gloves. "You're right, of course, my mistake." She looked up at him and the look in her eyes hit him hard. It was like a nasty belly blow from someone who's not fighting fair.

"I suppose that has been my problem from the very beginning," she said. "I have either overestimated or underestimate you and for that, I'm sorry."

"What are you doing here, Amelia?" He braced himself. "I thought your father had you under lock and key."

"My father knows I'm with Maddie," she said. "So what if we're an hour or two farther out than he thinks." She paused and put her hand on his arm. It raised an alarm that rang through him. "Truth be told, I came looking for you."

"I won't give up the stallion." He said the words almost as a gut reflex. She didn't even blink.

"I no longer want Applegate."

It was worse than he thought. "Then what do you want, Amelia?"

She bit her bottom lip. Darn it, she looked so pretty and smelled so good it took all he had not to grab her and kiss her and make promises he shouldn't ever make. Promises he wasn't sure he could keep.

"Amelia?"

"Alex." She took a step toward him. "I came to apologize for everything. I should never have forced you to marry me. I know that now, and I should never have tried to change you." She took a deep breath and pressed on.

The temptation to hold her, to touch her, to kiss her was so strong he was breaking into a sweat. He leaned back in his own defense.

"I just wanted to tell you that I think you are a good man, Alex Laird. That you are perfect just the way you are."

She took hold of his hand and placed something in his palm, then closed his fingers around it. Whatever she had given him was made of wood and still warm from her grasp. "I came to tell you that you won the game." Then she reached up and kissed him full on the mouth.

The kiss was short and sweet and filled with the promises his heart wanted to hear. It shocked him down to his toes. "I hope you find it in your heart to forgive me, Alex. I hope that someday you find yourself in love and that when you do, you will be happy. Because you deserve to be happy, Alex." She gave him a final sweet smile. "That was all I wanted to say. Good-bye, Alex."

She turned and hurried across the street. He opened his fist and looked down. She had filled his hand with match-sticks. The realization stung him. They were the matchsticks she had won in their card game.

He watched her as she walked away. She had just given him the unconditional love he had asked from her. What had she said? That he was a good man just the way he was.

Something inside him burst. She had found him in the meanest of saloons, gambling, and still . . . still she had handed over her heart.

It scared the heck out of him. What exactly did it all mean? Did he dare to dream?

He crushed the matchsticks in his hand and went after her. "Amelia!"

She stopped in the center of the road. A large wagon passed between them. His heart pounded in his chest. His head was light.

"Amelia," he said again when he reached her. "What are you saying?"

"I'm telling you that I love you, Alex," she said gently and placed her palm on his cheek. "It doesn't matter to me who you choose to be, what you choose to do. As long as I have breath in my lungs, I will always love you."

"But the annulment . . ."

"I told you before, I don't want an annulment. So, I will never file for one." She withdrew her hand. "It's okay if you don't love me," she said softly. "I won't file for an annulment, but neither will I block it should you file." She gave him a small, quick smile. "I will leave it up to you."

She stepped away. He grabbed her by the elbow and turned her to him. "What about your dynasty?"

"I don't care about that anymore," she said. "I don't care about anything but you. That's why I said I hope you find love. Because being loved by someone who loves you back is the biggest treasure in all the world. Good-bye, Alex Laird."

She walked away.

She walked away and he stood there with matchsticks in his hand. He glanced back at the saloon. He'd been winning but he still had been miserable. Then Amelia had come and told him that she loved him and now it was up to him to do something with it.

For a brief moment, Alex felt stark terror. He couldn't let her go. It was all her doing of course. After all, she had come back.

He ran after her and caught her just before she went into the mercantile. "Amelia, wait."

She turned, with love in her eyes, and something even better . . . hope.

"Amelia, I have already found someone to love. Don't you see?" He put his hands on her arms. "I love you."

"You love me?"

"Yes."

"Then why did you let Papa take me?"

"I loved you so much that I gave you your freedom."

"My freedom?"

"Yes, I wanted you to be free to marry the man of your dreams, which clearly is not me."

"Oh, Alex, you are so wrong. I don't want my freedom, silly man," she said and did the most remarkable thing. She reached up on her tiptoes and kissed his forehead, his eyes, and his cheeks. "I love you, Alex Laird. Gambler, farmer or dirt poor merchant, it doesn't matter."

"What about your dream of a horse farm?"

"Don't you see?" she said and grinned at him. "Married women can own property now. So, as long as you don't mind, I can pursue my dream with you at my side."

"So, *you* will be the horse farmer?"

"Yes, if it's okay with my husband."

He shook his head. "You're a nut."

"I know, but I'm a nut who loves you just the way you are. So, what do you say?"

"I've been miserable without you."

"Then you don't want an annulment?"

"Let's go home, Amelia." He kissed her. The future still scared the heck out of him, but it no longer looked so dark. "Go on then, get your sister. We'll show her our house."

"Oh, about . . . the house . . ." She stopped and turned to him. "Alex, I'm so sorry for changing around your house. If you like we can build a little cottage."

"For what? To store my stuff?"

"No, to live in."

"Amelia, it's okay. You were right. The house is so much better when it is used as a home. I have an auctioneer coming in on Monday to sell off everything."

"Really?"

"Yes, I figured there was no use letting all those things waste away in storage or, worse, wait for more robbers." He kissed her temple. "I plan on using the money to invest in breeding stock, but we could use it to renovate the nursery if you'd rather."

"Breeding stock?" She covered her mouth with her gloved hand. "Nursery?"

"Yep," he said. "Someone recently convinced me to try my hand at raising horses."

"Really?!"

"Sure. Seems to me it's as big a gamble as poker and you know I like to gamble. Maybe we'd better put some money into the nursery. No harm in being prepared."

"Oh, Alex," she said. "I love you so much."

He squeezed her hand and looked down into her shining eyes. "Thank you for loving me," he said. "I love you too. Now let's get your sister and go home."

They went happily, and Alex was as certain about their love as he was about his luck. With Amelia, he could conquer the world.